Break Free

From Emotional Distress

A Practical Guide and Personal Journey

Stephen Middleton, PhD

Dedicated

To my family… past, present, and future

Praise From Readers of *Break Free From Emotional Distress*

Dr. Stephen Middleton masterfully blends storytelling, wisdom, and personal insight into a compelling guide on resilience and self-worth. His authentic and insightful memoir leads readers on a powerful journey toward emotional and psychological freedom. He instills hope, faith, and determination through poignant stories and thoughtful guidance. More than just a book, *Break Free from Emotional Distress* is a masterclass in overcoming life's challenges. Please read it, embrace it, and take your first step toward breaking free!

Dr. Eleanor Hooks, Executive Coach and author of *I Am Well Where It Really Matters: Meaning From Cancer*

****

Dr. Stephen Middleton's *Break Free from Emotional Distress* is a powerful blend of courage, wisdom, and authenticity. Drawing from personal experience and well-researched insights, it offers a practical guide to overcoming emotional struggles. It illuminates the path to self-acceptance, resilience, and healing with strength, faith, and deep understanding. It is a must-read for anyone seeking transformation and personal growth.

Manuel Jose Muros, Transformational Guide and author of *The Other Side of Me: A Journey Into The Mystical & The Gems Revealed*

****

Break Free from Emotional Distress is one of the most raw and resonant books I've read. As someone who's worked in mental health for years, I've seen how heavy emotional pain can be. This book captures that weight and the quiet hope that follows. I was moved by Stephen's vulnerability, courage, and the raw honesty woven into every page. His journey through grief, trauma, and healing reflects what many of us carry but rarely articulate. This book not only normalizes emotional distress; it also offers wisdom, compassion, and practical tools to help readers find peace within their pain. I saw myself in many of these pages, and I know others will too. It's a rare book that meets you where you are and still dares to lead you somewhere softer.

Rashida Ruwa, RN, HDip Psych Nursing, Health & Wellness Writer

****

Break Free From Emotional Distress by Stephen Middleton, PhD, is a powerful testament to human resilience. Blending personal narrative with practical guidance, Dr. Middleton offers a deeply insightful journey toward healing and self-discovery. His compassionate wisdom provides solace, strength, and a clear path to emotional freedom. More than a guide, this book is a beacon of hope for anyone facing mental health challenges. I wholeheartedly recommend this transformative work to those seeking inner peace and empowerment.

Anna Yusim, MD, Clinical Assistant Professor, Yale Department of Psychiatry and author of *Fulfilled: How the Science of Spirituality Can Help You Live a Happier, More Meaningful Life*

Acknowledgments

Writing this book requires both transparency and vulnerability. One of the most challenging decisions I faced was sharing my life with readers. Another was deciding whether my experiences would resonate with others and offer value to those facing emotional distress and everyday challenges. I was encouraged by the insightful feedback of several individuals who helped me refine this book and gave me the confidence to publish it.

I am grateful to Rashida Ruwa, who took time from her psychiatric nursing practice to read every chapter and provide invaluable reflections. Anna Yusim, a psychiatrist and professor, generously invested her time to offer thoughtful feedback. Eleanor Hooks, an executive coach and author, made space in her demanding schedule to review my work and share her insights. Manuel Jose Muros, a yogi, author, and spiritual teacher, graciously offered his perspective, even as he navigated the major transition of relocating to another country.

I also appreciate my children's thoughtful reflections and encouragement. Their support made all the difference. Geraldine Benjamin, a retired teacher, read the manuscript and helped me catch errors, strengthening the final copy. Finally, the editors at Fawcett Publications played a crucial role in refining the prose, making this book a more engaging and insightful read.

To all of you, I extend my deepest gratitude.

Table of Contents

Preface

Weeping may endure for a night, but joy comes in the morning. Psalm 30:5

There are three inspirations for a personal self-disclosure book about mental health, a taboo subject in American, if not world culture. The first involved my number one brother, who passed away in 1995. Louis was battling lymphoma, a devastating cancer that had taken a toll on his body. When I visited him in the hospital that summer, the treatment had robbed him of his mobility. As he lay in his hospital bed with his elbow down, he raised a clenched fist, calling my name, saying,

I've learned so much from life, I can write a book.

He must have thought I wasn't listening. Staying with the same pose—elbow down on the bed with the clenched fist in the air, he called my name again, repeating the words:

I've learned so much from life, I can write a book.

Not knowing what else to say, I mumbled encouragingly, "Write the book." A few days later, he was gone. My brother waited until his final moments to realize he had countless life lessons to share, lessons he wanted others to learn from. Like him, I've gained valuable insights from my own experiences, and I'm sharing some of those lessons in this book to further your growth and understanding.

When you're struggling emotionally, you often search everywhere for relief. That's precisely what I did in the early 1980s, desperately reaching for anything to end the pain. Prescription drugs and talk therapy weren't enough. I grappled with thoughts that, in hindsight, seem trivial—like feeling that people didn't like me. But at the time, those thoughts consumed me.

They marked some of the bleakest days of my life. I felt isolated and alone. Alongside medication and regular visits to a psychiatrist, I frequently reached out to a mental health helpline at the hospital to feel connected to another human being. I remember the long nights when I couldn't sleep, the constant fear and anxiety that gripped me, and the struggle to find a reason to keep going.

When traditional methods failed to ease my emotional pain, I turned to movies and books. One film, *Uncommon Valor* (1983), starring Gene Hackman, stirred something deep within me. Hackman's portrayal of Colonel Jason Rhodes, a retired Marine Corps officer who led a team of veterans on a mission to rescue soldiers from a Vietnamese POW camp in Laos, resonated with me on a personal level. Their courage, dedication, and drive reached into my soul, making me feel I could not give up.

The 1984 film *Against All Odds* also resonated with me, primarily because of its title. It suggested a seed could rise from the mud and blossom into something beautiful even in the most adverse conditions. This movie instilled in me the belief that I could rise again, even when the odds were stacked against me.

Furthermore, I found another lifeline in a public library. As I browsed the shelves in the self-help section, I came across a little book, *Notes to Myself: My Struggle to Become a Person*, first published in 1970. Seemingly, the energy in the book called out to me, and it began to settle me the moment I placed it in my hands. *Notes to*

Myself is a profound personal disclosure book written by Hugh Prather. He provides a raw and unfiltered examination of some of his questions about the meaning of life and his daily struggles to find balance. By opening up about his fears, self-doubts, relationships, and uncertainty, he created a pathway for the rest of us to make meaning of our lives.

To Prather's surprise and likely delight, *Notes to Myself* struck a chord with readers everywhere. It opened a door for us to candidly share our innermost fears and concerns about life. From its pages, we know we're not alone, no matter what we face.

A promotional piece states, "Each note serves as a poignant mirror, encouraging us to embrace our imperfect humanity and ponder the silent questions that shape our existence." Prather's reflections resonate deeply, opening a pathway to a profound personal understanding of ourselves, our human journey, and our world.

I could not report most of the book's content when I left the library that day. Looking back, I know my mood improved; the book

gave me a sense of how human I was and offered the possibility of feeling better.

I hope *Break Free From Emotional Distress*
is such a book. Hence, I share my life and journey over the past 70 years as of 2024 with this
in mind. I hope someone who needs it finds it
and gets the feeling I had when I read *Notes to
Myself*. The first chapter establishes the foundation for the rest of the book. Readers can use
the table of contents to navigate to any section.
Each chapter has sufficient overlap to provide
context for the book.

From my experience, it contains enough
information to help anyone struggling with
painful thoughts. The book is also interactive.
Many chapters include exercises, and work-
sheets are provided at the end. Of course, you
may write inside the book, as I provide space
for your reflections. However, I suggest you
grab a notebook to record your thoughts.

My story is one of struggle, resilience, and
hope—a journey shaped by anxiety and depression but defined by perseverance and transformation. Born in the segregated South in 1954,
I came into a world where the odds were
stacked against me. State laws kept whites and

blacks apart, and like many Southern black children, I spent my childhood picking cotton and plowing fields with a mule.

But this is not just a story of hardship. It is a story of faith, hard work, and refusing to let circumstances dictate my future. It's about finding the strength to keep moving forward, even when quitting seems easier. From the dusty fields to the halls of academia, I made the journey from plowman to professor, all while battling the weight of anxiety and depression. It's a story worth telling, pointing out that others can also *Break Free*.

Chapter 1

Everyone Gets Dirty

Nobody is perfect. We make mistakes. We say the wrong things. We do the wrong things. We fall and get up. We learn, and we grow. We move on because that is life. Internet

Have you ever had a casual conversation with a stranger that became a profound learning experience? It happened to me many years ago. I have a physical disability that aroused the curiosity of someone I met at a banquet. My new dinner companion, let's call her Theresa, introduced herself as a holistic health practitioner in Applied Kinesiology. While eating a delicious meal and listening to calming music, she asked if she could test my muscles.

Theresa hoped to relieve my discomfort and release a cascade of healing. I appreciated her genuine concern for me and willingness to share her knowledge and expertise in holistic health. Our dinner companions watched as she practiced her techniques on me.

She mentioned that she had seen great success with individuals using muscle work and herbal remedies to alleviate chronic pain and improve mobility. This sparked my curiosity and made me eager to learn more about holistic approaches to managing my disability. I agreed to pursue her suggestions for alternative treatments and natural remedies that could help improve my health.

Everyone Gets Dirty

As Theresa chatted away, she casually mentioned that *everyone gets dirty as they move through life.* I did not understand what she meant, but now, decades later, I have a sense that she was talking about herself. She had had a full life of ups and downs and shared her truth. Theresa emphasized the importance of accepting the messiness of life, including our imperfections.

Everyone has something to learn from life, and my new friend wanted me to understand that everyone goes through the school of life—the school of hard knocks. Her wisdom continues to resonate with me on my journey.

When we are experiencing emotional distress, it is easy to think we are alone. We believe we are the only ones who make mistakes. When Theresa said that everyone gets dirty, she *normalized* life for us and invited us to consider that we all are part of a human family.

Normalizing our experiences liberates us from the illusion of perfection, transforming our mistakes into stepping stones rather than burdens. Theresa's words cut through the noise, reminding us that imperfection isn't just human; it's transformative. It's a shared thread that connects us all. Owning our flaws doesn't just build strength; it forges resilience, ignites confidence, and equips us to face life head-on, unfiltered and unapologetically.

However, most people who struggle with their mental health do not view life in this way. We see ourselves as unique and adopt the false belief that we are the only ones to have experienced adversity. We get hung up on seeing some things as good and others as bad. Often, we develop the habit of thinking that more bad things have happened to us than good things. We seem wired to look at the negative.

Psychologists Paul Rozin and Edward Royzman referred to this thinking pattern as "Negativity Bias" in a 2001 article. They argued that we give more weight to the negative without consciously thinking about it. As we go about our daily lives, it becomes easy to overlook the good we have done and let our mistakes overshadow them. We develop the habit of seeing life events from this biased perspective. People in emotional distress tend to see themselves in this way.

We see ourselves through the lens of being broken. However, we must remember that our mistakes and flaws do not define us or determine our worth. It is necessary to practice self-compassion and acknowledge the good we have done, especially in times of emotional distress.

Theresa knew there was power in recognizing that everyone gets dirty and *normalized* life for us all by asserting this unalterable truth. When you are suffering, you are most likely oblivious to this maxim. But to live in peace, you must discover that you are just like other human beings, doing your best. When people are unaware of this, they suffer from negative self-talk that might sound like this:

- *I am the only one who made this mistake in life.*
- *I am the most foolish person alive.*
- *You would reject me if you knew what I did.*
- *I cannot take this psychological torture any longer.*
- *I'm such a foolish person.*
- *If I had that choice to make over again, I would do it differently.*

When you have these thoughts, they will exert long-term "phantom power" over you. However, it is not real power; it is only what you take as reality. Phantom power feels real—when you entertain hurtful thoughts, they can grow until they leave you feeling dysfunctional.

Many people who suffer fail to recognize that our thoughts shape our feelings. It is not about what you have done or what has happened to you; it is about how you think about those experiences. Acknowledging that mistakes and failures are normal and essential can transform your mindset.

When you practice self-compassion, embrace your imperfections, and recognize that life is a journey of learning, you can experience profound personal growth. By shifting from blame to seeing mistakes as opportunities, you can *break free* from the cycle of self-condemnation and adopt a healthier, more positive way of living. Recognizing that everyone makes mistakes will empower you to move forward confidently and have compassion for yourself.

Negative Self-Talk

Do you ever catch yourself in the grip of hurtful self-talk? It's easy to overlook how automatic these thoughts have become. These negative beliefs may have been "looping" in your mind for years, perhaps even decades, continually shaping your inner narrative without your awareness.

Let's pause and take a bold first step: write down four of your most stressful thoughts. By identifying these recurring patterns, you strip away their power and challenge the lies they've fed you for so long. This process demands honesty and courage, but it has the potential to reshape your mindset and free you from their hold. It's a chance to reclaim your strength, rebuild your perspective, and take ownership of your life.

Take stock of your stressful self-talk by listing four of them:

1. _______________________ 3. _______________________

2. _______________________ 4. _______________________

If you've taken a moment to write down your hurtful thoughts, you've probably noticed something—they're the same ones that have haunted you for years. It's shocking and freeing to realize this: no new stressful thoughts exist. As Byron Katie, author of *Loving What Is* puts it, "They are all recycled." Talk to a group of people, and you'll discover many of them are wrestling with the same inner battles, replaying the same tired scripts in their minds.

I've seen it in my own life. During a virtual workshop, I joined a small group focused on facing reality instead of clinging to fantasies of how life "should" be. What struck me wasn't just the vulnerability of the group but how familiar their stories felt. Although we came from different countries and spoke different languages, our struggles were remarkably similar. Their understanding and compassion hit me deeply, reminding me that I mattered. On the surface, we were strangers, but beneath it all, we were the same, walking parallel paths.

This is the reality: you are not alone. Your struggles aren't unique punishments designed just for you. They are part of the human experience we all share. Knowing this isn't just comforting. It's powerful. It reminds you that others are fighting alongside you, chasing the same clarity and peace. Let that connection "ground you." *You're not alone, and you never were.*

People in emotional distress often believe their self-talk defines them, mistaking these thoughts as reflections of their identity. Looking back, recalling when I first tried to change my hurtful self-talk nearly fifty years ago is almost amusing. Like everyone else, I naturally tended to have a negative bias, but I was unaware of it then.

My journey began when a friend introduced me to Wayne Dyer's book, *Your Erroneous Zones: Step-by-Step Advice for Escaping the Trap of Negative Thinking and Taking Control of Your Life*. However, the ideas seemed completely foreign to me back then, almost as if the book had been written in a language I didn't understand.

The issue was not the book itself—Dyer's insights were profound. The problem was my inability to grasp his message at that point in my life. It was as if my emotional pipes were clogged, just as the pipes in your home can be blocked. However, that awareness of my negative self-talk ignited a desire to find solutions.

My search continued until I discovered Ziglar's *See You at the Top*, a truly inspiring work in self-help. While Ziglar's words resonated more with me, I understood that the journey to overcoming negative self-talk is deeply personal. What works for one person may not work for another, but the right solution is out there for each of us, waiting to be discovered. And it is the calling of your life to seek until you find it.

Overcoming negative self-talk wasn't straightforward. It was a battle fought inch by inch. At first, I thought I had to argue with every thought, break it down, and prove it wrong. But that only gave those thoughts more power. Eventually, I realized the truth: I didn't need to fight them. They were like background noise, always there but meaningless unless I decided to listen.

So, I stopped listening. Not all at once; it was just for a few seconds at first. But those seconds stretched into minutes, hours, and then entire days. It wasn't some grand epiphany but a gritty, frustrating process of choosing not to let my mind run the show. And with every choice, I felt the grip of those thoughts loosen. They didn't disappear, but they stopped running my life. That was the real win.

This practice taught me that I could co-exist with my thoughts without allowing them to define or control me. Through persistence, I gradually began to see these thought patterns as harmless noise. I stopped steering them toward positivity and instead tuned them out altogether. That shift transformed my experience of my inner world. And with perseverance, you can too.

When you commit to this process, you will discover that we all have hurtful thoughts. The power lies in choosing whether to let them disturb us or not. With time, you will cultivate awareness and the ability to let those thoughts exist without allowing them to define or control your life.

Don't lose hope if your journey to improve your life hasn't yet worked out. And don't allow past experiences with therapists or psychiatrists to make you feel like healing isn't possible. It's not your fault, and it's not theirs. Sometimes, the right path just hasn't appeared—until now.

Your struggles don't define you, and they don't mean you're beyond help. What they mean is that your breakthrough hasn't come yet. But that moment could be now. Together, we can uncover the tools, the mindset, and the strength to finally move forward. You deserve joy, healing, and peace—not someday, but starting right here, right now. Let's begin.

Experts on Emotional Suffering

For centuries, thinkers and philosophers have taught us that our thoughts often trouble us more than the events themselves. The Greek philosopher Epictetus captured this perfectly when he said, "Men are disturbed not by things, but by the views which they take of things." This emphasizes the power of perception; how we see a situation determines its impact. Nothing is inherently good or bad; our thoughts make it so.

William Shakespeare echoed this idea with his famous line, "There is nothing either good or bad, but thinking makes it so." Even something as profound as death is not universally seen as negative. Epictetus explained that Socrates, another Greek philosopher, rejected the fear of death, saying, "But the terror consists in our notion of death, that it is terrible. When, therefore, we are hindered, or disturbed, or grieved, let us never impute it to others, but to ourselves; that is, to our own views."

In our time, Dr. David Burns continues this exploration of the mind, emphasizing that mood disorders like anxiety and depression often stem from the way we think. According to Burns, our thoughts create our moods, particularly when we bombard ourselves with negative messages.

This cycle of self-blame and judgment can make us feel worthless and even physically ill. Burns, author of several books, including *Feeling Great*, has trained thousands of professionals to help people recognize that negative thinking is often the root of their struggles.

Similarly, Sydney Banks, a twentieth-century spiritual teacher, taught that while thought is not reality, it is through thought that we create our realities. Neuropsychiatrist Dr. Abraham Low, a pioneer in the self-help movement, reinforced this idea, stating that "Feelings are not facts. They lie to you and tell you of dangers that are not real." In essence, when we are caught in a negative mental state, we are not seeing reality clearly, though our distorted thoughts may feel profoundly real.

Negative self-talk is a common struggle that people everywhere face, regardless of their background or identity. Many of us hear those hurtful voices and accept them as truth. But it is not the thoughts that hold us back; our attachment to them causes suffering.

The key to breaking free is recognizing these negative thoughts for what they are: distorted perceptions, not facts. We take away their power by challenging and refusing to agree with their false messages. Pair this with practicing self-compassion and filling your mind with healthier, more rational thoughts, and you begin to shift the narrative. This isn't just about silencing negativity but reclaiming control and moving toward a more positive, empowered mindset.

The Source of Your Thoughts

This exercise may help drive home the point and help you recognize where your hurtful thoughts originate. It is easy to think that your feelings come from circumstances or personal history. You might say, I grew up in the wrong family or lived on the wrong side of the tracks, which is why I feel the way I do. You may also say that you made too many mistakes to feel better—if you had only done fewer stupid things in life, you would not feel this way.

No one should be traumatized by anyone, and if you have been hurt, I am sorry. We will deal with trauma later, but let us consider the possibility that past trauma cannot harm you now. By engaging in these exercises, you will understand how your thoughts impact your emotional well-being, not where you grew up, your circumstances, or your trauma.

Once you become aware of this, your healing has begun. You will learn how to change your thought patterns, allow them to pass on by, and enhance your mental clarity. From this, you will naturally experience greater happiness, and your well-being will flourish. You can learn to reframe negative thoughts by considering other possibilities and adopting more positive and constructive explanations for your experiences.

This experiment will reveal the source of your thoughts. I adapted this technique from Cindy Teevens, a spiritual teacher living in Canada. Cindy is an author and maintains an active presence on social media. To help you gain insight into her process, I will walk you through where you think sound comes from. Your thoughts are like sounds. They come from the same place. Once you realize this, you will immediately gain power over your thoughts and know their origins. This single recognition can significantly improve your mental well-being and quality of life.

Exercise

Preparation: Grab the device you use to play music and pick a song you like. Find a quiet place where you can sit comfortably without interruptions. Have your device ready to play music when prompted.

Activity: Once you choose your song, play it at a comfortable volume. You can close your eyes to minimize distractions or keep them open while listening to the music. Allow yourself to get into the music.

Reflection: As you listen to the song for a few minutes, write down your thoughts about where the music originated. Describe any emotions or memories the song evokes. Use the space below to write your responses; there is no right or wrong. I will not test you or ask you to see it my way. I only request that you answer my question about the origin of the music.

Questions to Ponder and Answer

1. Where do you hear the music? Identify two places. Is the music coming from another room? Which room?
2. Can you manipulate the music (e.g., can you grab it and put it in a closet?)? What happens to it when you try to grab it?
3. Is the music originating in space? Where else is it coming from?
4. Are you listening to music from outside yourself? Yes or No (circle one)
5. Are you listening to music inside yourself?
6. Yes or No (circle one)
7. Are your thoughts originating outside yourself? Yes or No (circle one)
8. Are your thoughts originating inside yourself? Yes or No (circle one)

Record your reflections on these questions in a journal or wherever you keep personal notes. Once again, there is no right or wrong. I will not test you on this exercise. The goal is to explore your thoughts and feelings freely and openly. Please continue exploring my questions and see if the music arises within you or from the outside. Remember, your thoughts come from the same place as the music you hear.

The Journey of Life

It's hard to see a way out when your mind is chaotic. Distress has a way of trapping you, convincing you that the problems never stop and the storm inside you will never calm. It's relentless. I know because I've lived it. I've felt that inner eruption; that mental war where peace feels like an impossible dream.

Cindy Teevens calls this a "stupid state," which is a contracted one, where all we assess are the limiting information in the mind (content and beliefs, as well as stories stored from the past) and relive it in the mind. When in this state, you cannot take in fresh, new, and alive thoughts; you stop accessing what's happening now, which is where intelligence lives. If you find yourself in a stupid state and suffering in the mind, pause, and try this activity. Cindy advises giving yourself five minutes to experience suffering as deeply as possible and stop unconsciously dreaming.

After five minutes, find something else to do. Dr. Abraham Low called this being objective, which can break your trance. It could be anything, including feeling your butt in a chair or walking across grass bare feet. Take a break and do whatever you can to free yourself from the grip of emotional distress. Focus on reality, and you'll discover you can terminate the noise in the mind.

A stupid state can pull you under if you let it. But here's the truth: you don't have to stay there. Even if you're drowning in emotional distress, self-doubt, guilt, or shame, there is a way forward. Brighter days are ahead; they're not just a hope but a reality. And when you find them, you'll experience a profound peace that defies understanding.

This isn't some clinical observation or secondhand advice. This is a raw, unfiltered account of someone walking through the fire. This book isn't research—it's lived experience, the hard-earned truth of someone who knows exactly what it feels like to be in that place. And if I can find my way out, so can you. I'm here for you. Let's do this.

Let us review some stressful thoughts:

1. *Regret* (I am sorry for my actions.)
2. *Fear* (I worry about not resolving my emotional suffering.)
3. *Hopelessness* (I worry that I can do nothing to feel better for more extended periods.)
4. *Self-doubt* (I have allowed my emotional state to stop me from doing some things.)
5. *Shame* (There are some things I have had trouble sharing because of embarrassment.)
6. *Guilt* (I am sorry about some things I have done.)

Can anyone have a peaceful mind if these concerns occupy their thoughts?

Now, it is your turn to list six stressful thoughts that bother you:

1. ____________________________

2. ____

3. ____

4. ____

5. ____

6. ____

I understand. You feel how you feel, but you may miss an important truth. As noted, Dr. Low told us we cannot trust our feelings. What can you learn from this? Do not trust your thinking when you are not feeling your best. I have learned the hard way that I should not make any critical decisions with consequences when I am experiencing emotional distress. You can always wait; if a choice is right, return to it when you're clearer and more rational. I will discuss decision-making in more detail in another chapter.

Because of my experience with emotional distress, I care about people who suffer. I have developed a proven method to help you find relief quickly. It is my secret sauce for alleviating emotional distress, if you receive it. Here it is: *Everyone faces daily challenges in this journey called life.* Do you remember Theresa saying: *"Every-*

one gets dirty?" She meant everyone! I say *Every-one faces daily challenges*, and I mean it! You are not alone. You must know and believe this truth without a doubt! It is not a slogan. It is a truth that cannot be altered.

To achieve mental serenity, you must *nor-malize* all aspects of your life, including positive and negative events. When you realize you are not alone, you have discovered one of the most crucial superpowers. You have *normalized* your life and become part of the human family. Al-low yourself to grasp it now and embrace the security that comes from it. Reading this state-ment is not enough, and I understand that. You must also absorb it and engage in a specific practice to help you integrate this message into your spirit.

To illustrate the practice of normaliza-tion, let's conduct another exercise. I want you to create a list of saints and sinners—achievers and failures, as you perceive them. Stay with me; do not give up or panic because of these words. I recognize that "sinner" may seem harsh, but when you suffer, you probably be-lieve you are beyond redemption. You think of yourself as a sinner. So, make your list, and be as thorough as possible. Do not sabotage your progress by saying things like this:

- *I cannot think of anyone whom I would consider a sinner.*
- *This exercise is too hard.*
- *This exercise makes no sense.*
- *What good will this do?*

These are all ways to fool yourself and sabotage your progress. As you create your list, record as much information as possible about the individuals, including their triumphs, weaknesses, and failures. If you already feel familiar with these individuals, it is crucial to learn more about them. This step is a suggestion and a vital part of your journey. You may include both the living and the dead on your list.

I have created a sample worksheet below to serve as a guide. Like me, I invite you to record the names of at least seven people you admire. On your list, create two categories to record their accomplishments and failures. You will notice that several of the names on my list are taken directly from the Bible. I grew up in a Christian home and attended church for

23

many years, so the Bible is buried in my soul. Growing up, I looked to the Bible for guidance from biblical characters, so these are examples of people who achieved great things but also made mistakes.

I also enjoy history; therefore, I draw inspiration from people in this field. The characters I use from the Bible and modern history illustrate their strengths and weaknesses. This is important because I want to *normalize* my life and use them as my guide. I invite you to do the same. Remember what Theresa told us: *everyone gets dirty*. Embrace this truth.

Though you are not required to do so, choose people you respect for your list. As you review my list, you will notice that I share the triumphs—the things I admire about the individuals on my list—and their flaws, those so-called blunders in life. I invite you to do the same. Additionally, refrain from trying to change yourself as you progress through this exercise. Do not try to ease your emotional pain. Let the process take care of it for you. All you need to do is complete the work: read the book and finish the assignments.

Regardless of your choice, I am confident this will help you feel better. I can say this because I experienced low emotional states as I wrote this book. I had self-doubt, feelings of regret, shame, and worry. Reading this chapter helped me release those emotions, and I am confident it will have the same effect on you. If you don't feel relief the first time you read it, don't despair. Read it again and again until you feel a sense of relief. If, for any reason, you cannot read it now, please put it away and return to it later.

Eventually, to paraphrase scripture, *suffering may endure for a night, but joy will come in the morning.* It is helpful to keep going, and the worksheet below will serve as your guide. Here is my sample worksheet. You will fill out your worksheet shortly.

Sample Worksheet

Moses: Hebrew Prophet and Teacher

Moses' Achievements: credited with leading the Israelites out of slavery in Egypt and across the Red Sea after God separated the waters; credited with taking the Israelites towards the "Promised Land;" credited with receiving the *Ten Commandments* from God; credited with writing Five Books of the Old Testament: Genesis, Exodus, Leviticus, Numbers, Deuteronomy.

Moses' Shortcomings: After God gave him his assignment, Moses didn't initially see himself as capable of leading Israel from Egypt. He lacked self-confidence and often doubted his ability as a speaker. Moses experienced anger. He killed a person to defend people he cared about. Moses disobeyed God and was not allowed to enter the Promised Land. Moses doubted God, despite having witnessed numerous miracles.

David: King of Israel

David's Achievements: He is credited with uniting the tribes of Israel, is the author of the Psalms, and displayed unusual courage and faith when he armed himself with only a slingshot to face a Philistine warrior named Goliath. He was also an accomplished musician and is described as "a man after God's own heart" in the Old Testament.

David's Shortcomings: King David abused his power by taking Bathsheba, the wife of Uriah, a man in his military service. When he discovered that Bathsheba had become pregnant, he conspired to deceive her husband, Uriah, by getting him drunk and sending him home, which the loyal soldier refused to do. King David involved his military leaders in a conspiracy to murder Uriah by arranging for him to be placed in a hot military battle, which led to his death. With Uriah gone, David married Bathsheba.

St. Paul: Apostle of Jesus and Bible Writer

Paul's Achievements: He dedicated at least 20 years to teaching and preaching about Jesus. He established several churches in Asia Minor and Europe. He wrote half (13) of the Books in the New Testament. He preached the gospel to Gentiles, which refers to non-Jews. Paul is widely regarded as one of the intellectual giants of his time because he encouraged people to think about God in new and innovative ways.

Paul's Shortcomings: Paul, a Pharisee, participated in the persecution of the early disciples of Jesus. He hunted them down and was complicit in their deaths, *i.e.*, Stephen, who was stoned. Paul played a leading role in attacking the church in Jerusalem, and his reputation for violence against believers was enough to send them fleeing for safety.

Dr. Martin Luther King, Jr.: Civil Rights Leader and Nobel Prize Winner

Dr. King's Achievements: Dr. King earned a Doctor of Philosophy degree in systematic theology from Boston University. He served as pastor at Dexter Avenue Baptist Church in Montgomery, Alabama, and Ebenezer Baptist Church in Atlanta, Georgia.

Dr. King led the Montgomery Bus Boycott, a pivotal event that helped spark the modern civil rights movement in the United States. He founded the Southern Christian Leadership Conference (SCLC), which fought for civil rights and equality for African Americans. He championed nonviolent resistance to counter white violence against blacks.

In 1963, Dr. King delivered his iconic "I Have a Dream" speech at the March on Washington, calling for a society where people are judged by the content of their character, not the color of their skin. In recognition of his efforts, he was awarded the Nobel Peace Prize in 1964 for his leadership and commitment to achieving racial justice through nonviolence.

Dr. King's Shortcomings: In his memoir *And the Walls Came Tumbling Down*, Reverend Ralph D. Abernathy, whom Dr. King considered his closest friend and confidant, acknowledged King's flaws, particularly his struggles with infidelity. Abernathy, who described Dr. King as his "best friend in the world," revealed that King had extramarital relationships, including some on the eve of his assassination. This revelation humanizes Dr. King, reminding us that even the most revered figures have their struggles.

Additionally, despite his remarkable courage, Dr. King faced tremendous pressures and threats from whites, which at times left him vulnerable to fear, despair, and self-doubt. In a rare moment of vulnerability, Dr. King said, "It seemed that all my fears had come down on me at once… And I got to the point that I couldn't take it any longer. I was weak." Nevertheless, his unwavering faith was a source of strength throughout his life.

Muhammad Ali: Humanitarian and three-time world heavyweight boxing champion

Ali's Achievements: Ali won the light heavyweight gold medal in boxing at the 1960 Olympics and became the Heavyweight Champion of the World three times, the first at 22. He was a civil rights advocate and opponent of the Vietnam War. He lost his boxing title and was convicted in federal court, but the Supreme Court later overturned the conviction. A humanitarian, he made a significant contribution to the world stage by supporting relief and development initiatives in impoverished areas.

Ali's Shortcomings: Although he was unaware of it, his difficulties in school, particularly with reading, were due to dyslexia. He had a reputation for his extramarital affairs and was married four times. He had seven children from these marriages, plus two daughters he fathered outside of marriage.

John Kennedy: President of the United States

Kennedy's Achievements: He ignited the United States' space program, which led to the first space travel in 1961. He established the Peace Corps in 1961 by executive order, pending congressional funding. He provided modest support for the civil rights movement. Kennedy also proposed civil rights legislation to guarantee equal access to public facilities, to end segregation in education, and to provide federal protection of the right to vote. He wrote *Profiles in Courage*, which won the Pulitzer Prize in history.

Kennedy's Shortcomings: He was rumored to have had ten extramarital relationships, allegedly including White House secretaries and a nineteen-year-old college intern. The president's most famous rendezvous was with the Hollywood beauty Marilyn Monroe, who, according to the movie *Blonde*, was frequently escorted to JFK by his Secret Service detail.

Oprah Winfrey: Media Mogul

Oprah's Achievements: After launching her career as the host of the award-winning The Oprah Winfrey Show, she founded the Oprah Winfrey Network. She is also the founder of O, *The Oprah Magazine*, and Harpo Films. President Obama awarded her the Medal of Freedom, the nation's highest civilian honor. Oprah rose from extreme poverty during her childhood in Mississippi to amass a fortune in the billions of dollars and is one of the most recognizable people in the world.

Oprah's Shortcomings: Due to no fault of her own, Oprah was sexually abused at age nine and was pregnant at the age of 14. After giving birth, the baby did not survive. She's also admitted that she made bad choices early in life due to the trauma she experienced.

You will undoubtedly agree that these people have gained international recognition. They were not flawless, but most people do not immediately recall their mistakes when they think of them. Rather than being discouraged by their misfortunes or errors, we are inspired by their gifts and attempts to help others.

If you feel you've made mistakes, you are not peculiar, out of the ordinary, or unique. As a human, you have been assigned this path that you call your life. It selected you; you did not choose it. It is yours to experience. In life, *everyone gets dirty*; it's time to accept it and *normalize* your experiences.

Worksheet

(Follow my format when creating your worksheet. You'll need to make the worksheet on a separate sheet of paper.)

Person 1: _______________________________
Achievements:
Shortcomings:

Person 2: _______________________________
Achievements:
Shortcomings:

Person 3: _______________________________
Achievements:
Shortcomings:

Person 4: _______________________________
Achievements:
Shortcomings:

Person 5: _______________________________
Achievements:
Shortcomings:

Person 6:_______________________________
Achievements:
Shortcomings:

Person 7: _______________________________
Achievements:
Shortcomings:

As I have said, I come from a Christian background. The gospels report that scribes and Pharisees, purportedly holy men, brought a woman to Jesus, whom they charged with bad behavior. Someone had caught the woman in the act of adultery. They wanted the woman stoned, under the law, but Jesus ignored them and wrote something on the ground.

When questioned further, Jesus replied: *He that is without sin among you, let him first cast a stone at her.* These men were better than some of our critics. They realized they also had missed the mark when they heard the truth. No one threw a single stone at this woman, nor did Jesus. It may be hard to grasp, but if your accusers are honest, they will not cast a stone at you. You must absorb this truth and breathe in its core message. *Normalize your life; everyone gets dirty,* including you.

Like the people on my list, you cannot change what has happened. You can't change "what is"; you can only learn from the past and accept it. Another book by Byron Katie, *A Thousand Names for Joy,* emphasizes that everyone can find joy in whatever life brings. Similarly, James, a writer in the New Testament, encourages us to consider all life experiences as joy. There will never come a time when you can undo an event in your life. Your only task is to embrace *what is,* again and again, until you discover an unshakable peace within yourself.

When emotional distress takes over, it's easy to turn against yourself, focusing only on your flaws while forgetting all the good you've done and continuing to do. Like the people I recorded on my worksheet and those on your worksheet, you also have achievements and shortcomings. The shortcomings do not make you bad; they make you human. As a reminder that you join the rest of us in having successes and shortcomings, take stock of some of them in this personal assessment below.

Personal Worksheet (Yourself)

List as many examples as you wish:

Achievements: _______________________________

___________________   ___________________

___________________   ___________________

Shortcomings: _______________________________

___________________   ___________________

You have strengths that set you apart and weaknesses that make you human—don't let either be ignored. It's time to stop dismissing your wins as "no big deal" or pretending they don't matter because they do. Your achievements prove the risks you've taken, the battles you've fought, and the impact you've made. They're yours, and they deserve to be celebrated. Own them unapologetically, because no one else will do it for you.

Gratitude List

When I was a boy in church, we learned a hymn called "Count Your Blessings." The choir repeated this refrain.

Refrain:
Count your blessings, name them one by one
Count your blessings, see what God hath done
Count your blessings, name them one by one
Count your many blessings, see what God hath done

Create a list of your achievements and express gratitude for what you are thankful for. Do not hold back; it is your time to recognize how you shine.

1. _________________________ _________________________

2. _________________________ _________________________
3. _________________________ _________________________
4. _________________________ _________________________
5. _________________________ _________________________
6. _________________________ _________________________
7. _________________________ _________________________
8. _________________________ _________________________

Do not stop if you have more to say. Recognize your good qualities and praise yourself. You were destined to have every experience you had. You are supposed to be where you are in life. Life is not about money, cars, clothes, houses, and land, even though enjoying the fruits of your labor is nice. You are here to learn because life is a learning experience.

A verse that circulated on the Internet in 2024 is a fitting way to close this chapter:

I hope you end the year feeling peace, not pain.
I hope you look back with gratitude, not regret.
I hope you accept the past and stay confident in the present. I hope you are ready to step boldly into what's ahead.

Chapter 2

Discovering Your Worst Day

Bad things are not the worst things that can happen to us. Nothing is the worst thing that can happen to us!
Richard Bach

Emotional distress is not caused by the bad things that happen to us. They are caused by the way we think about them. To underscore the point, *your suffering does not stem from the external events in your life but from the way you interpret those events.* This distinction is crucial.

We have all encountered trauma in one form or another, whether it is from the trauma of birth, being bullied on the school playground, or facing a violent crime. Experts often categorize trauma as "Big T" (severe, life-changing events) and "Small T" (more subtle but still impactful life events). Thankfully, the human spirit is remarkably resilient, and many individuals who have endured extreme suffering have gone on to heal and move forward.

However, it is essential to realize that the emotional pain you feel is not necessarily tied to the worst event you have ever had. Personal experiences, while painful, are not the sole cause of emotional pain; how we think about those experiences plays a more significant role. Understanding this is the key to overcoming what is currently holding you back.

Reframing your thoughts can help release the emotional weight holding you back. I will share my journey through painful experiences that once held me back. From my sharing, I hope you will realize that adversity does not have to become a life sentence. It can become an opportunity for growth and transformation.

In *What Happened to You? Conversations on Trauma, Resilience, and Healing*, Oprah Winfrey and Dr. Bruce Perry explore how trauma, whether significant or subtle, shapes our lives. While Oprah is a household name, Dr. Perry is an expert in childhood trauma and is known for his work helping children heal. In his previous book, *The Boy Who Was Raised as a Dog*, Dr. Perry shared stories of children facing unimaginable hardships and highlighted their remarkable resilience.

What Happened to You? dives deeper into the lasting impact of trauma, illustrating how our life experiences, big or small, can affect our psyche, sometimes even unconsciously.

Oprah claims the book holds "the key to reshaping our very lives," acknowledging the importance of understanding the events that shaped us. Rather than asking, "What's wrong with me?" we are invited to ask, "What happened to me?" This shift in perspective opens the door to healing, offering clarity and the potential for profound personal transformation.

Let's take a moment to pause and reflect on your life—not to dwell on the past, but to gain a deeper understanding of it. Think of yourself as a storyteller piecing together the moments that shaped who you are today. I'm not here to reopen old wounds or invite you to dwell on them. This isn't about pity; it's about perspective.

When you reflect on those stressful moments that leave a lasting impression, you gain a broader perspective. These moments, what I like to call the "environmental factors" of your life, have shaped how you think, feel, and act. But here's the thing: you're not stuck in that story. When you take the time to understand these events, you gain the power to change the narrative.

I'll go first. I'll share my story to heal myself and illustrate that you're not alone. We've all been shaped by something—pain, love, loss, growth—and those experiences don't have to define us forever. They can teach us, guide us, and even push us to become something more.

Environmental Factors

Do not underestimate the significance of environmental factors on your mental health. Even as a layman, I can predict a person's feelings based on the conditions that shaped them. Your environment might crush you and leave you in despair for a long time or serve as a catalyst for developing resilience and growth. It all depends on how you perceive and respond to the challenges in your surroundings. There were several moments in my life when events hurt, but you may be surprised that some of them are not the things that trouble me the most.

In October 1996, my world shifted in a way I could never have prepared for. My first son, Steve, passed away suddenly at just sixteen years old. The pain still feels raw, but what I hold on to most is who Steve was, not just as my son but as a person.

Steve had this way about him—he was the kind of guy you couldn't help but like. Friendly, easy-going, and full of life. He used to joke that he was "an all-around nice guy," and honestly, Steve was. Everyone who knew him would say the same. Whether on the football field or hanging out with friends, Steve always cheered people on, made them laugh, or was there when they needed him.

Steve wasn't just a big-hearted, jolly guy; he was tough, too. A natural athlete, he excelled in football, particularly on the offensive and defensive lines. I remember that during his physical for the season in August, the doctor told him he was "strong as an ox." That wasn't an exaggeration. He was a member of the 300-pound club, lifting weights as if it were nothing. However, what truly set him apart was his exceptional leadership. On the field, he didn't just play; he led. He had this way of encouraging everyone around him, pushing his teammates to keep going, no matter how tough the game got. He once told me, "If they can hold on to the runner, I will bring him down." And you better believe he would. That was Steve—determined, dependable, and full of promise.

One crisp October morning, we sent Steve off to school, unaware it would be the last time we'd see him awake. That afternoon, during football practice, Steve collapsed while doing drills. EMTs arrived quickly and rushed him to the emergency room at a nearby hospital. From there, they transferred him to the Trauma Center at a university hospital. We clung desperately to hope, praying for a miracle that never came.

A compassionate nurse, with a quiet sadness in her voice, gently told us what we couldn't bear to hear: Steve might never leave the hospital. In the face of the unimaginable, my wife and I made the agonizing decision to remove him from life support. Telling our other children and Steve's friends that he was gone was like breaking our hearts all over again.

There are no words to describe the pain of losing a child; it's a soul-deep wound that never truly heals.

As painful as it was to bury my son, I also felt an inexplicable energy during that time—a presence that assured me his life, though short, was complete. Although I still feel a twinge of sadness today, I also feel a sense of peace. I can smile at the memory of his infectious spirit or shed a tear because he is no longer here. But I no longer dwell in sorrow. My understanding of death has helped me find solace—I know I was not at fault, and I have learned to let go of the unbearable pain.

The Death of My Father and Brothers

I lost my father in 1978, creating a void that can't be filled. At just 24, I barely began to know him as an adult. Leaving home for college at 18 meant we missed the chance to connect as men. My children never met him, and I have often grieved the missed opportunity to see him bond with them.

The 1990s brought more losses. I've already mentioned the death of my son in 1996. Before then, in 1992, my second brother passed away at 42. To honor his life, I wrote a poem that seemed to flow through me. Sadly, the complete poem is lost, but this verse is representative of it:

Although your body is in the ground,
I know you are with God.
How do I know?
I can feel you in the wind.
I can see you in the twinkle of the stars.

Three years later, in 1995, my first brother passed away at just 48 years old. We shared many years, but I still mourn the loss of what we didn't get—a chance to grow old as brothers. When I see siblings past fifty laughing, reminiscing, and enjoying life together, it's a painful reminder of what could have been.

Thankfully, my immediate family had a period of reprieve from the angel of death. But a few decades later, I lost my mother and one of my sisters. Each loss cut deeply, carving out parts of my soul I will never get back. The death of loved ones leaves wounds that time softens but never truly heals.

As if the losses weren't enough, life threw another challenge in my way—my health. In 2008, a routine PSA test turned my world upside down with a prostate cancer diagnosis. I'll never forget that Sunday evening call from my doctor. The moment I heard the word "cancer," it felt like the ground beneath me had shifted. Grief hit like a tidal wave, but there was no time to drown in it.

Treatment began quickly with seed implants to target the cancer cells, and for a while, it seemed like the nightmare was over. But in 2011, the cancer returned, and this time, I had to undergo cryotherapy. Thankfully, the treatments worked, but the emotional toll was far more challenging to overcome. Hearing "cancer" changes you in ways no one prepares you for.

Yet, that wasn't the only battle I had to fight. Another health challenge has lingered in the background for decades, slowly chipping away at me. It began in my early thirties with something as subtle as a slight waddle in my walk. Over time, muscle weakness and mobility problems worsened. Today, I can no longer stand tall or lift my arms as I used to.

The initial diagnosis was limb-girdle muscular dystrophy, but later, it was reclassified as unknown muscular dystrophy. I've sought answers from some of the world's leading medical institutions, including the Mayo Clinic and Duke University, but no effective treatment has been found. All I've been given are assistive devices like my walker and power chair to help me adapt to a body that feels less and less like my own. It's a quiet, invisible kind of trauma—one that's hard to explain but impossible to ignore.

Despite the losses, the grief, and the relentless health struggles, I've discovered something powerful within me. These challenges have tested me, but they've also revealed an inner strength I didn't know I had. Life hasn't been easy, but I've learned to face it with determination, to find peace in chaos, and to hold on to gratitude and hope even in the most challenging moments. The human spirit is stronger than I ever realized, which keeps me moving forward.

Growing Up

Growing up often leaves scars that can take a lifetime to understand and heal. My childhood in Cross, South Carolina, was no exception. Cross, a quiet rural community about fifty miles northwest of Charleston, had all the country charm you'd expect—scenic views, with Lake Moultrie winding its way through the landscape. But beneath that beauty was a harsh truth: poverty. To say we were poor feels like an understatement. Many families in our community shared the same struggle, but that did not make it any easier.

Our home was a modest, flimsy frame house—more patchwork than structure. We had just one small wood stove to heat the entire house, which meant winters were fierce. Our bedroom had two glass windows with broken panes. A heavy blanket covered one, and a shutter nailed over the other. Neither could keep the biting cold out.

At night, I'd lie in bed and stare at the stars through the holes in the tin roof. During the day, sunlight streamed through cracks in the floor, revealing the sand beneath. Rainstorms were an ordeal—buckets and pots were scattered throughout the house, trying to catch the steady drips from above.

Life was a constant battle for survival. Yet somehow, we never went hungry. Our meals may have been born out of necessity rather than choice, but they sustained us. We made do with what we had, finding a way to get through each day.

Cross as a Family

Despite our hardships, Cross was more than a place—a community that felt like one big family. Neighbors looked out for each other, and acts of kindness were commonplace. One of my cousins introduced me to church and Sunday School. Those Sunday mornings were transformative. I loved summarizing lessons before the congregation, a practice that nurtured my lifelong love of the Bible and learning. Decades later, as an adult, I became a Sunday School teacher, carrying forward the lessons that shaped me as a child.

Living in Cross also taught me the power of a positive mindset, thanks to my uncle. He was a neighbor and an extraordinary mentor who shared wisdom with anyone who would listen. When I doubted myself, he reminded me, powerfully in his broken English, "Can't been dead; I helped bury the scoundrel!" Moreover, when I worried that circumstances would hold me back, he told me, "Take what you got, and make what you want."

Beyond words, he taught me practical skills—how to hammer nails, saw wood, and even slop hogs. Once, he took me to a local merchant and bought me a pair of khaki pants, my first piece of new clothing in a long time. The merchant, glancing at my worn clothes, asked my uncle, "What kind of shirt do you want for the boy?" My uncle answered without missing a beat, "You must have read my mind." The merchant replied, "No. I just looked at the boy."

Acts of generosity like this were woven into the fabric of life in Cross. When my father killed a hog, neighbors helped with the butchering and left with a piece of meat. Families shared vegetables and groceries when someone was in need. When my parents decided to add two rooms to our home, men from the neighborhood volunteered their labor, and women gathered to quilt blankets. Though we had little, we had each other, which made all the difference.

My Parents

My parents planted crops on our plot, and we worked as sharecroppers for others. One of my earliest memories is lying on a sheet at the edge of a cotton field while my mother worked. As I grew older, I joined her in hoeing cotton fields and vegetable gardens. We shuck cornfields and pick cotton. By the time I was 14, I could pick over 100 pounds of cotton in a day—a source of pride in our household. At 16, I inherited the mule and a plow while my brothers found work as general laborers in the construction industry.

Our home life came with challenges beyond poverty. We lacked indoor plumbing, adequate heating, and basic amenities. The first time I bathed in a tub was at 14, during a visit to my sister in New York. By the time I was 18, as a college student, I had finally experienced the luxury of regular showers. Of course, these circumstances were not unique to me because most families in Cross lived as we did, lacking the basic facilities we take for granted today.

My parents worked tirelessly to provide for us. My father supported eight children, a monumental task I can barely fathom as a parent of three. He worked at a lumberyard until the owner fired workers for organizing a union. Undeterred, my father found a new job in sanitation in a nearby city and worked there until his death. Though my father struggled with alcohol, drinking corn whiskey from Friday to Sunday, he was always up for work on Monday. He never cursed, whipped, or mistreated me. His love was quiet but steadfast, expressed through his dedication to providing food for his family.

My mother was ambitious and business-minded. In 1972, she transformed our family's fortunes by discovering a program through the U.S. Department of Housing and Urban Development (HUD) that helped families build new homes.

Taking the initiative, she handled the paperwork while my father's job qualified him for the loan. As I left home for school that fall, my family moved into a new four-bedroom brick house with central heating and plumbing. It was a monumental change. My mother kept the house after my father's passing in 1978 and paid off the mortgage in her lifetime. It remains in our family as a testament to her courage and determination.

Lessons from Cross

Growing up in Cross left me with more than memories of hardship; it gave me a deep appreciation for community, determination, and the power of hope. From neighbors who shared their bounty to a family that worked tirelessly for a better life, I learned that kindness and determination can create abundance even in the face of scarcity. Those lessons remain with me, shaping how I see and strive to improve the world.

Racism and Fears

Racial segregation defined the South during my youth, a reality that deeply shaped life in South Carolina. In our small community, I rarely saw white children, and families of other races didn't live nearby. Skating rinks and the drive-in movie in a nearby town were private clubs for members only, which meant whites.

Our high school band played in Christmas parades as some whites painted their faces black, to mimic the sambo character from an earlier time. The Sambo caricature portrayed black people as lazy, docile, and clownish, reinforcing racist stereotypes used to justify their subjugation.

Public schools remained segregated until the fall of 1971, when Berkeley County schools were officially desegregated. Even then, most white families opted to send their children to private academies, leaving only a handful of white students in our high school. Calling it integration would be an overstatement. This was the environment I grew up in—a society divided and defined by race.

Reflecting on *What Happened to You?* by Oprah Winfrey and Dr. Bruce Perry, I often think about how my early life, filled with countless "Small T" traumas, shaped who I am today. But even more, I wonder about the generational trauma that shaped my parents and their parents before them and the lingering shadow of slavery that followed black families into the 20th century.

My parents, born in the 1920s, and their parents, born around the turn of the century, endured the harsh realities of segregation and systemic oppression. My father never attended school, and my mother only reached fifth grade. Their parents, deliberately excluded from education, could not read or write, bearing the weight of a society that denied them basic humanity and opportunity.

The trauma of racial violence and systemic oppression was woven into the fabric of our lives. Hearing my sister talk about being chased by the Ku Klux Klan was heartbreaking. My father's habit of referring to a white man as "captain" left an indelible mark on me, as did my encounters with racial discrimination.

As a boy, I worked clearing land at Rocks Pond Campground in Eutawville, South Carolina. The supervisor refused to call us by name, addressing us as "dillies"—a slight improvement from the N-word. My brother and I also worked for a Klansman and merchant who objected to us taking a lunch break. When we protested, he called us "African chimps." Though we walked off the field that day, the sting of those words lingered.

Night Sweats and Impostor Syndrome

From an early age, I lived with an overwhelming fear of the dark, an anxiety so intense it caused night sweats and heart palpitations. My father's ghost stories may have sparked my fears and perhaps the emotional strain of my environment. The fear manifested in various ways. In my mid-teens, I believed I saw a ghost walking into a pond near a relative's house, which made me panic.

On another occasion, a cousin refused to walk me home after band practice, leaving me to sprint home in terror as my heart seemed to pound out of my chest. Once, a church member dropped me off far from home, thinking it would "toughen me up," but the experience only deepened my fear. Looking back, I wish an adult had talked to me about this abnormal fear and helped me neutralize it.

Lacking self-confidence was another significant challenge I faced. Many of my peers from Cross High School went on to achieve successful careers in business, education, law and medicine. Yet, I often felt like an impostor, especially as I stepped into college, graduate school, and, eventually, the workplace. That persistent voice of impostor syndrome—the feeling that I didn't truly belong—followed me everywhere, making me question my abilities and downplay my achievements. It became a constant source of anxiety and even depression.

My educational journey was particularly challenging. Coming from a rural background, I found it difficult to fit in at elite universities. While some professors were encouraging, others were harsh and dismissive, reinforcing my self-doubt. During my master's program, a professor suggested I pursue a doctorate but also voiced doubts about my writing skills due to my early education. Years later, while supporting my promotion at work, he reiterated his opinion, telling me he never considered me a strong writer.

The criticism didn't stop there. During my doctoral program, some professors suggested that my writing lacked the clarity of thought necessary for academic success. Their words stung, leaving me feeling inadequate and unsure of my place in the academic world. Even in a post-doctoral program, I faced harsh feedback. A professor in a legal history seminar criticized my work so severely that it brought me to tears.

The irony? That paper, torn apart in the classroom, later won a best-article award from a historical society. It was a bittersweet moment, a poignant reminder of how easily we can internalize criticism and undervalue our potential, even in the face of undeniable success.

As a university professor, I often felt isolated. I was frequently the only black professor in my department, and some colleagues made subtle remarks about my perceived intellectual deficiency. Despite my efforts, I could never measure up in their eyes. Students occasionally questioned my competence, and department heads used student evaluations to criticize my teaching effectiveness. These experiences compounded my impostor syndrome and reinforced feelings of inadequacy.

These challenges, however painful, have shaped who I am today. They have allowed me to reflect deeply on my life, understand their influences, and grow from them. I encourage you to reflect on your experiences, as I have. This is not about self-pity but about gaining clarity and wisdom. Acknowledging what happened to you is the first step toward healing and empowerment.

Free Write Exercise

Summarize some of your experiences with the following topics in mind. Use a separate sheet of paper if you have more to say about your life.

Your community: ________________________________

____

____

____

____

Parents: ________________________________

____

____

____

____

Positive Experiences: _____________________

____

____

____

____

Adverse Experiences: _____________________

____

____

____

Psychoeducation

Taking stock of your early life can be one of the most empowering things you'll ever do. The wisdom you gain from this reflection can unlock healing and spark transformation. It's not just about knowing what happened; it's about understanding how it shaped you and why it still matters. To move forward, you have to uncover what still bothers you today.

This is where psychoeducation can help. Psychologists use it to teach clients and their families about the stressors that shaped their lives, helping them understand and process those experiences. It's not about clinging to past hurts; it's about gaining clarity and letting go of what no longer serves you. You've likely heard the saying, "Knowledge is power," or the scripture, "With all thy getting, get understanding." These phrases reveal the same truth: we look back to move forward.

The Akan people of present-day Ghana have a concept that embodies this idea perfectly. It's called *Sankofa*, which means "go back and fetch it." The translation emphasizes that it's never wrong to return to the past for something you've forgotten or left behind. Sankofa reminds us that wisdom from our past is essential for growth. The symbol for Sankofa, a bird looking back while holding an egg in its beak, is a beautiful reminder of this profound truth. Reflecting on your life and asking, "What happened to me?" is more than just a starting point—it's an active, essential part of the healing process.

When I look back on my own life, I see that, although some experiences have been painful, they do not define who I am. I've experienced tremendous losses of my son, siblings, and parents. I've faced serious illnesses and lived with a debilitating condition for which there is no cure. I've endured decades of professional challenges. But none of these events control my identity or my peace of mind. I can acknowledge the sadness of those moments without being consumed by suffering.

Here's the thing: most people don't suffer solely because of their hardships. Everyone faces challenges at some point in life. Emotional suffering comes not from what happens to us but from how we interpret and internalize those experiences. The stories we tell ourselves about our pain, the way we replay and personalize those moments in our minds, create suffering.

If trauma inherently caused suffering, I would have spent years trapped in despair. But

I'm not. Instead, I've learned that how I process what happened—thinking about it, framing it, and assigning meaning—determines whether I experience peace or pain. I've realized that some things I found most troubling then wouldn't even faze most people. This reinforces the idea that suffering isn't about the events but how we mentally frame and respond to them.

Therefore, psychoeducation is a tool that can begin to reshape patterns of emotional distress. It can give us the knowledge and understanding to interpret our experiences more effectively. Through the power of reflection, we can release emotional suffering and move toward healing and peace.

On the other hand, you'll experience emotional suffering if you live with thoughts like the following:

1. *I am sorry I did that thing. (Guilt)*
2. *I wish I had been more mindful and made better choices. (Regret)*
3. *I would live differently if I could do it over. (Forecasting, Regret)*

4. *My life would be better if I hadn't had that experience. (Forecasting)*
5. *I am embarrassed when people discover my past. (Shame)*

Are any of these concepts familiar to you in your self-talk? If you are experiencing emotional pain, I surmise you have had them or some version of them. But I have good news for you: they are not the truth. They are all lies coming from your mind. Some energy vibration came your way, and you believed them. That is the only problem.

Listen, some people have experienced terrible events and lived happily and freely afterward. Many people do not get stuck in the story. We do not forget the trauma; we learn to live with it in a healthier way that no longer causes emotional suffering. It is like living with the death of a loved one. We do not forget it or get stuck in the story about losing them.

I am writing this book because I believe I have found answers to heal my emotional suffering, which has lingered for decades. Let me be clear: I do not write as one who has already attained, but as one who presses toward the mark, just as Apostle Paul said in the New Testament. My stories and scenarios are from the laboratory called *My Life*.

I will explore my story in greater detail in other chapters. For now, it is your turn to reflect on some of the trauma in your life. Do not hold back; you do not have to share your list with anyone. Remember, my list included the deaths of my eldest son, my parents, two brothers, and a sister, mobility challenges, and prostate cancer. I also mentioned how these events made me feel. It would help if you did the same: do the work.

Exercise

What happened to you? Be specific and avoid writing sentences. ______________________

____

____

____

____

How did they make you feel? List your Emotions. ______________________

____

____

____

____

Bad Things Happen to Good People

I am genuinely sorry for the pain and challenges you've faced. Life often presents experiences that defy understanding, leaving us to grapple with one of its most profound questions: *Why do bad things happen to good people?*

Many senseless events globally puzzle us, and we have no answer for why they happened. I'll share three stories close to my heart that are etched in my mind, compelling me to ask *why bad things happen to good people.*

One involves a young woman who underwent surgery for a medical condition unrelated to her legs. In a tragic mistake, the surgeon amputated both limbs. She had no history of diabetes or illness affecting her legs. There was no logical reason for the surgery, which was unrelated to her original diagnosis.

She eventually won a malpractice lawsuit and was awarded a large payout. However, no amount of money could restore her legs. She now lives with prosthetics and questions that have no answers.

In another shocking story, a 16-year-old boy living with an abusive stepfather woke up in the hospital completely blind. His stepfather had shot him, rupturing the optic nerves in his eyes. He had to relearn how to navigate life from the perspective of a blind individual. He graduated from college and earned a master's degree. His transformation was so complete and powerful that he now says being blind is the best thing that happened to him. Now, at 58, he reflects on his journey as he writes and shares his story with reporters and podcasters.

Lastly, a college student and ROTC officer had envisioned a career in the military. He was also a gifted athlete who had excelled at football since high school. After pledging a fraternity, he looked forward to a bright future. During a St. Patrick's Day event with his fraternity brothers, he stood watching the parade when an altercation erupted nearby. Gunfire rang out, and a stray bullet struck him. He awoke weeks later in the hospital as a person with paraplegia. At his lowest moment of despair, he begged his parents to let him go, but they couldn't bear it. Now kept alive by a ventilator and fed each meal, he remains tethered to his bed. Yet he writes books, appears on podcasts, and shares reflections on life and gun violence through social media.

These stories, and many more like them, remind us of how fragile life can be and how suffering often defies logic. They often leave us searching for meaning in chaos, grappling with the question, "Why did this happen to me?"

Authors and theologians have grappled with the complexities of human suffering, offering insights to help us navigate these challenging times. Ken Yabuki's *Why Bad Things Happen to Good People and What Can Be Done About It: A Christian Perspective* highlights how adversity can become an opportunity for spiritual and emotional growth. Similarly, David Arnold's *Why Bad Things Happen to Good People: Answers to One of Life's Greatest Moral Questions* explores how suffering can reveal God's ability to bring comfort and healing.

Harold S. Kushner's *When Bad Things Happen to Good People* stands out as a deeply moving reflection on coping with his young son's devastating illness. His insights remind us we can find meaning and strength even in pain. Other authors, such as Brent L. Top, Derek Prince, and Shaul Rosenblatt, share their wisdom, reminding us that suffering is a universal experience that connects us all.

Instead of asking why bad things happen, consider this perspective: challenges are inevitable. Personal trials, however painful, are an integral part of human existence. Accidents occur, natural disasters strike, and tragedies affect people worldwide. It is a harsh reality, but one worth acknowledging: this is life.

When you face a challenge, try to *normalize* it—not to dismiss the pain, but to remind yourself that you are not alone in your struggles. Reflect on this question: *Would you trade your experience for someone else's?* The idea may seem tempting at first, but think carefully. Are you sure you want the life you think someone else has? I pray you never end up with the burden you imagine to be "better" than your own or the life you believe to be free of hardship. Trust me, you would not want mine.

If you have not done so, watch the 1983 movie *Trading Places* with Eddie Murphy (Billy

Ray Valentine) and Dan Aykroyd (Louis Winthorpe III). It is a comedy, but it carries a valuable lesson. In the story, two wealthy brothers, Mortimer and Randolph Duke (played by Don Ameche and Ralph Bellamy), wager on whether environment or heredity shapes a person's character. To test their theory, they orchestrate a role reversal between Valentine and Winthorpe, forcing each to experience life through the eyes of another individual.

Now, I'm inviting you to try a similar exercise. Imagine trading your burdens with someone you admire. Take a sheet of paper and divide it into two columns. In the first column, list your current struggles. In the second column, write the name of someone you would hypothetically trade places with—someone you think has a more enjoyable or better life. Be honest. As you learn more about their life, you might find their challenges as real and heavy as yours.

This exercise is not intended to minimize your pain, but to help you gain perspective. It reminds us that every life carries its unique burdens, and what we imagine to be easier often is not. Embrace your journey, with all its difficulties, knowing that you're not alone—and that growth usually comes through our struggles.

Trading Places

Who Would You Give Your Burden?
Person: ________________________________
The Burden? ________________________________

Whose Burden Would You Accept?
Person: ________________________________
The Burden: ________________________________

Is it clear that we all have burdens and encounter challenges and adversities? Instead of dwelling on their unfairness and assuming that someone has it better than you, focus on learning and growing from your experiences. You may discover that nothing in your life was good or bad. It is just how life unfolds for you at any given moment.

You will have to reach the end of whatever you are facing, including the end of life itself, to see how things worked out and perhaps recognize how your life is better because of your experiences. Events in our lives are not the problem. We have power over how we experience life, and we get to choose that experience.

Your Journey Is Your Assignment

No one picks their journey in life. At first glance, this may seem like a strange statement. After all, we talk about free will and the power of choice—and we do have options—but our circumstances often shape and inform them. Have you ever heard the expression, "I wish I had known this yesterday"? The truth is, you did not know yesterday, and that is why you could not make a different choice then.

Life is a learning experience, and the lessons you need will inevitably come your way. You cannot avoid them; it is *cosmic law*. Ramesh Balsekar was a spiritual teacher deeply rooted in the Advaita Vedanta tradition, teaching the *cosmic law*. He said cosmic law operates beyond human understanding and that life unfolds according to a divine, impersonal order, or a universal law. Specifically, Balsekar explained that there are:

- *No Individual Doer*: Individuals are not the doers of their actions but rather live under a cosmic law driven by conditioning and circumstances.

- *Acceptance of Reality*: He urged us to accept life as it is, without resistance or blame, since Universal Intelligence governs them.

- *Impersonal and Perfect Order*: Cosmic law ensures that everything in the universe happens precisely as it should. While this order may not align with human notions of justice or fairness, it operates perfectly within its framework.

- *Freedom from Guilt and Blame*: Recognizing that actions are not personal liberates individuals from guilt for their actions and blame toward others.

Balsekar encouraged living in harmony with this law by cultivating surrender, trust, and non-attachment to outcomes, understanding that everything arises and dissolves within the grand flow of existence.

Would Balsekar's teachings help you live a lighter life? For years, I struggled with regret and thoughts about how things might have been. However, this burdensome way of viewing life changed when Balsekar gave me a new transformative perspective: *My experiences were unavoidable because they were part of cosmic law.* This was my assignment, designed to shape my understanding of the world. They gave me a unique lens through which I now view life, a perspective that has become the foundation of this book.

As I noted earlier, I grew up in a rural community under challenging circumstances. My family was poor, and my parents, who had eight children, were illiterate. There were no books or magazines in our home. In the 1960s, it was common for boys in my community to drop out of high school, and my brothers followed that path.

However, I chose a different route, undoubtedly, because it was part of my assignment: it was *Divine Law.* I pursued higher education, eventually earning a master's and doctorate. Over nearly four decades, I served as a university professor, was the inaugural director of an academic program for ten years, and lectured at two universities in the United Kingdom. I have written multiple books and numerous articles. Few individuals would have predicted this outcome when I was born in 1954. However, as life's path unfolded before me, I followed it. It is a story I share with a thankful heart.

If I can accept that this journey was chosen for me, why shouldn't I also accept the painful parts of my life? Even in those moments, I resisted and disliked them because they, too, were preselected. Balsekar's teachings helped me see that resisting life's painful moments only deepens suffering. The root of emotional pain lies not in the experiences themselves but in our refusal to embrace them as part of the grand design. They are a part of *cosmic law*. Through acceptance, I have found a lighter way to walk through life.

But the recipe for a burdensome life comes from thinking like this:

- *I dislike this experience.*
- *If I had better advisors, life would have turned out differently.*

- *If that person had not entered my life, I might have avoided this pain.*

These thoughts are all illusions. Everything had to happen as they unfolded, and nothing could have saved me from the adversities I faced.

If I could request an exemption from the traumas in my life, it would not be from the most painful or lingering experiences that have weighed on my mind. Instead, my plea would be for my son to live. I would endure a lifetime of suffering if it meant having my son with me. Yet even his death, as devastating as it was, was not my deepest wound. My path—woven with the good, the bad, and the ugly—was mine to follow. This is the paradox of life: the pain we would never choose is often intertwined with the love we would never trade.

Assess Your Journey of Life

Are there experiences you wished you could have avoided? List them below:

1. ______________________________________
2. ______________________________________

3. _______________________________
4. _______________________________

Who do you think you would be without your life experiences? Free Write your reflections. Use additional pages as needed.

____
____
____
____

What are some of the positives in your life experiences exactly as you have lived them? Free write your reflections below. _______________

____
____
____
____

In 2024, I entered my eighth decade of life. If there is one truth I have learned, it is this: *you cannot change the past.* Whatever your reality is now—that is it. You can move forward but never backward. It is *cosmic law.*

I admit that I've watched too much TV over the years, but I picked up a valuable lesson about the past from the TV show *24,* starring Kiefer Sutherland as Jack Bauer. In Season 7, there is a gripping moment involving Jonas Hodges (Jon Voight), the head of Starkwood, a private military company responsible for domestic terrorism and the death of President Allison Taylor's (Cherry Jones) son. Despite Hodges' heinous crimes, he had critical information that could help the president uncover a larger conspiracy brewing in the capital. Reluctantly, Taylor granted him a presidential pardon.

This decision enraged Olivia Taylor (Sprague Grayden), her daughter, who could not stomach Hodges walking free after her brother's death. Fueled by grief and anger, Olivia contacted Martin Collier (Leland Orser), a shadowy operative, to arrange Hodges' assassination. Collier warned her that once this happens, you can never go back. However, Olivia was determined, claiming she wanted Hodges killed. Then, in a moment of frantic regret, Olivia tried to undo her decision, but Collier bluntly reminded her of her prior decision and said that *the time to change your mind had passed.*

This scene powerfully teaches us about regrets, doubts, and self-recrimination: *once something has happened, it is over.* There is no going back. You cannot rewrite what has already been written. This is the reality of your life, and I urge you to live it to the fullest and for your highest good.

One final thought: if there is someone with whom you can make amends, do it. While reconciliation is not always possible or necessary, the best way to honor a fresh start is by living your best life from this moment forward. Let your actions today reflect the person you aspire to be, not the one you were yesterday.

Exercise

What is the one thing from your life you want to change? _______________________________

____

____

____

____

Free write your reflections about the thing you want to change: _______________________

____

____

81 _______________________

____

Wrestling with your past may be your only difficulty. I will address the past more fully in the next chapter. For now, a verse circulated on the Internet in 2024 may underscore the point:

Never regret a day in your life. Good days give you happiness, bad days give you experience, worst days give you lessons, and best days give you memories.

Chapter 3

The Past is Like a Shapeshifter

I count not myself to have apprehended, but this one thing I do, forgetting those things which are behind, and reaching forth unto those things which are before, I press toward the mark for the prize. Apostle Paul

Our emotional struggles often originate from how we hold onto and interpret memories, especially those tied to unresolved conflicts or emotional pain. Heavy with regret, perceived missed opportunities, or unspoken words, these memories can linger in our minds, casting long shadows over the present. They shape not only how we see ourselves but also how we view others and the world around us, quietly influencing our choices and interactions.

The human mind fixates on what went wrong, replaying moments of failure or hurt like a broken record. This constant rehashing reinforces negative emotions and keeps us stuck in patterns of self-doubt or sadness. Over time, these persistent thoughts can do more than weigh on our feelings—they can disrupt our nervous system, keeping it in a state of high alert or chronic stress.

It's like a pot of water simmering on a hot stove—if left unchecked, it eventually boils over. Similarly, unresolved emotions can overwhelm us, creating a sense of being emotionally and physically stuck. But understanding this connection between our memories, feelings, and physical responses is critical to breaking free.

By acknowledging the impact of these lingering stories, we can begin to rewrite the narrative. This shift helps restore balance and empowers us to approach life with greater clarity, peace, and understanding.

The Shifting Nature of Memory

Let me share a personal story that taught me how a seemingly simple event from the past can distort our perceptions in profound ways. Back in high school, my school employed student bus drivers. The supervisor in charge, aware of my family's financial struggles, offered me a chance to join the team and earn some extra money. It was a kind and generous gesture, but there was one problem: the driving test conflicted with band practice. At the moment, I chose the band.

At first glance, this might seem like a small, insignificant decision, but it became a source of regret that weighed heavily on me for years. I blamed my band teacher for not excusing me from practice and wished someone—a parent or mentor—had guided me through the decision. The truth, however, was that only the supervisor knew about the opportunity, and no one else had the context to step in. Yet I unfairly distributed blame—to others and myself.

What started as a simple scheduling conflict became much more significant to me. It became a symbol of self-doubt and the moment that made me question my judgment and decision-making ability. For years, I carried this regret as proof that I couldn't get things right.

Looking back now, I see how I had transformed this minor event into a defining moment of failure. This experience highlights a challenge we all face when revisiting our past: our memories are not static. They shift and warp depending on our emotional state, like shadows stretching and shrinking as the sun moves.

Something small and fleeting can grow disproportionately in our minds, feeding our insecurities and reshaping how we see ourselves and the world around us. My key lesson was learning to view these memories with perspective—not as verdicts on who I am, but as moments that don't define my entire story.

The Nervous System

Ryan North, a trauma expert, co-founder of One Big Happy Home, and creator of The Empowered Parent Podcast, states, "Our brains are wired for connection, but trauma re-wires them for protection. That's why healthy relationships can be complicated for individuals who are wounded." However, we often overlook the nervous system in our daily lives. This intricate network is constantly at work behind the scenes, the unsung hero that keeps us healthy and alive.

Let's take a moment to become better aware of its significance. The nervous system serves as the body's communication hub, orchestrating everything from voluntary actions, such as walking, to involuntary ones, like heart-beat or digestion. It's a two-part system: the central nervous system (CNS), which comprises the brain and spinal cord, and the peripheral nervous system (PNS), a network of nerves that extends throughout the body. These systems enable us to think, move, feel, and maintain balance.

But what happens when this delicate system becomes imbalanced? The consequences can be significant. An unhealthy nervous system can manifest in various ways—brain fog, memory issues, or strange sensations like tingling and numbness. Stress, poor diet, or exposure to harmful substances can disrupt the system, leading to more severe conditions like neuropathy or even multiple sclerosis. And here's a crucial point that many overlook: the nervous system isn't just about physical health; it's deeply intertwined with your emotional well-being.

When life throws us into chronic emotional distress, like feeling stuck in regrets or replaying past mistakes, the nervous system reacts. Your body shifts into survival mode, keeping you in a fight, flight, or freeze state.

This constant state of alarm doesn't just weigh on your mind; it can also make your body feel out of balance. You might notice yourself feeling exhausted, on edge, or unable to concentrate. Over time, this imbalance can leave you feeling like your emotions are running the show, and your body isn't far behind in following suit.

There is good news. You can restore balance to your nervous system. The first step is to recognize that the nervous system is at the core of this struggle; it's not that you're broken or beyond repair. This realization can be profoundly healing.

From there, simple practices such as deep breathing, mindfulness, and gentle exercises can help guide your nervous system out of stress mode and into a calm state. When you allow your body to relax, you also create space for your mind to heal. Over time, this can transform your relationship with your past and help you embrace the present moment.

Learning from Science Fiction

As a longtime *Star Trek* fan, I've immersed myself in nearly every show the franchise has offered since the original series, many of which I've watched multiple times. These shows transcend entertainment, offering rich storytelling, moral dilemmas, and deep explorations of human nature.

As a viewer and a student, I draw insights from *Star Trek*'s lessons about navigating life and understanding our relationship with the past. *Star Trek* offers a unique blend of science fiction and timeless wisdom about how identity, memory, and growth can be transformative.

The series frequently examines how characters confront their histories, choices, and regrets, revealing how the past can shape us, both as a source of strength and a barrier to further understanding. It demonstrates how engaging in our past can empower us to move forward or cause us to get stuck in despair.

In this section, I'll share four powerful examples from the *Star Trek* series that illuminate different aspects of our human journey. Perhaps these moments will enrich your understanding of how art offers practical lessons for your life as they do mine. They highlight universal truths that resonate far beyond where no one has gone before, addressing themes like regret and guilt and reclaiming the agency necessary to navigate life.

The Past in Star Trek: Original Series

The original *Star Trek* offers a profound exploration of interpreting the past in "All Our Yesterdays." In this episode, Captain James Kirk (William Shatner), Commander Spock (Leonard Nimoy), and Dr. Leonard "Bones" McCoy (DeForest Kelley) visit a doomed planet. The star Beta Niobe is on the verge of exploding, and the away team arrives to warn the inhabitants.

However, they soon discovered an unusual escape mechanism: a media room overseen by Mr. Atoz (Ian Wolfe), the planet's librarian. This room contains disks that serve as gateways to other worlds—a means for individuals to flee for refuge in another period. Unbeknownst to the Starfleet crew, most inhabitants had already used this method to escape.

In a twist of fate, the crew members are inadvertently separated. Kirk is transported to Cromwellian England, while Spock and McCoy are sent to the Ice Age. Spock begins to lose his characteristic Vulcan stoicism in harsh Arctic conditions. His emotions, long suppressed by logic and discipline, reawaken to a primal state. His encounter with Zarabeth (Mariette Hartley), a woman exiled to this frozen world, catalyzes this transformation. Lonely and vulnerable, Zarabeth forms a deep connection with Spock. For a fleeting moment, Spock contemplates abandoning his responsibilities and staying with her.

However, McCoy—recovering from a paralyzing illness—recognizes Spock's emotional changes and urges him to return to their mission. When Kirk called them back to the library, the spell was broken, and Spock reluctantly returned to the media room. Once reunited in the present, Spock's humanlike emotions receded, yet McCoy wondered if the weight of his experience lingered. Reflecting on the encounter, he stares at Spock; assessing his state of mind, Spock exchanges poignant words with him about the past:

- *Spock*: There's no further need to observe me, Doctor. As you can see, I've returned to the present in every sense.

- *McCoy*: But it did happen, Spock.
- *Spock*: Yes, it happened. But that was five thousand years ago. And she is dead now. Dead and buried. Long ago.

The power of Spock's realization lies in his acceptance of an immutable truth: the past is unchangeable. While his connection with Zarabeth was genuine, it belonged to a time long gone, Spock acknowledged, and dwelling on it would only hinder his ability to live fully in the present. It may have also disrupted his nervous system, causing a perpetual imbalance of sorrow.

This message resonates universally. Whatever has happened in your past is as unchangeable as history itself. Like Spock, we must learn to move forward, letting go of the things we cannot change. Embracing the present moment and making peace with the past enables us to rewire our brains and live more fully in the present. Allow Spock's mantra to guide you: *The past is dead and buried; only the present moment remains.*

Remember, a different life doesn't come from erasing the challenges or so-called mistakes of your past. This profound idea is brilliantly illustrated in *Star Trek: The Next Generation*'s Season 6 episode, "Tapestry." In this story, Captain Jean-Luc Picard (Patrick Stewart) faces an unusual twist of fate when an accident during an away mission kills him in a dream as he lies on *The Enterprise*, fighting for his life. In the dream, Picard awakens in an afterlife, where he encounters the mischievous and omnipotent Q (John de Lancie), who has shadowed him many times.

Picard met Q as God and reflected on his life, where he expressed regrets about the brash, selfish, and reckless young man he once was and regretted some of his decisions. This scenario invites us to relate to the moments we believe have tarnished our lives. Q, seizing the opportunity for amusement, offers Picard a second chance to rewrite his past and avoid those mistakes. Like many of us, Picard is determined to correct his youthful impulsiveness, choosing a safer path: he avoids conflict, takes fewer risks, and adopts a cautious demeanor as a Starfleet cadet.

However, this new life comes at a heavy cost. By playing it safe, Picard sacrifices the qualities that made him an inspiring leader. His old friends lost respect for him, and his career stalled. When this alternate version of Picard arrives aboard the Enterprise, he finds himself in a low-ranking, unremarkable position. Far from the confident and decisive captain we know, he is seen as timid and uninspiring, an officer unsuited for leadership.

Desperate to reclaim his former self, Picard confides in Commander William Riker (Jonathan Frakes) and Counselor Deanna Troi (Marina Sirtis), expressing his frustration and longing to contribute meaningfully to The Enterprise. Though kind, they were blunt in their assessment: Picard lacks the boldness and authority essential for command. The realization hits him hard, shattering his self-image and leaving him reeling in remorse.

At his lowest, Picard ultimately pleads with Q to undo the changes he had made, declaring that he would rather die as his flawed, daring self than live as the hollow man born of his safer choices. His plea carried the weight of a lifetime of experiences and the wisdom gained from them. Q, moved by Picard's self-awareness, restores him to his timeline. He awakened back aboard *The Enterprise*, alive but with a scar on his chest, a physical reminder of a near-fatal fight from his youth. Laughing and grateful, he embraces his messy, imperfect life.

The episode imparts a powerful lesson: our mistakes and hardships are not detours but essential components of who we are. They forge our character and give us the strength and wisdom to grow. Picard's journey teaches us not to rewrite our past but to accept it. Life's triumphs and challenges shape us into the unique individuals we become.

Wisdom from Star Trek: Voyager

Star Trek: Voyager presents another opportunity to grapple with notions of a painful past. One show that resonates deeply with me is Episode 105, *"Latent Image."* In this powerful story, the holographic physician, "The Doctor" (played brilliantly by Robert Picardo), faces a harrowing moral and emotional dilemma. The Doctor is confronted with a heart-wrenching decision: to save the life of Ensign Ahni Jetal (Nancy Bell) or Ensign Harry Kim (Garrett Wang).

Both are equally deserving, yet The Doctor chooses to save Harry, his friend. This choice shatters his programming, plunging him into an existential crisis. As he grapples with the repercussions of his decision, The Doctor begins to unravel, questioning his very essence and morality.

In seeking to protect him, Captain Janeway (Kate Mulgrew) initially deletes the corrupted files containing his deflated personality. But she is encouraged to recognize his humanity—his right to wrestle with pain and grow from it—just like the rest of her crew. Janeway allows him to face his trauma head-on.

The Doctor's transformation reaches its peak when he reflects on a verse from Dante Alighieri's *La Vita Nuova*: "In that book which is my memory, On the first page of the chapter that is the day when I first met you, Appear the words, 'Here begins a new life.'"

His realization that life is a collection of memories, even for him, a hologram, becomes his turning point. He had been holding onto his trauma, trapping himself in a cycle of perpetual suffering. But he discovers a profound truth: *every moment is an opportunity to start anew.* The refrain "Here begins a new life" becomes his mantra—a powerful reminder that rebirth is always within reach.

The Doctor's message is not just for him but for all of us. No matter our circumstances, we all have the power to start anew. A fresh beginning doesn't always arrive with fanfare; sometimes, it comes quietly—in an hour, a day, or even a single breath.

I've carried this philosophy into my life, even in small, everyday moments. For example, I once ordered the wrong clothing size online and fretted over the mistake. Instead of spiraling into frustration, I took the necessary steps to resolve it and released the worry. Fretting over the past wouldn't change the outcome, but embracing the present moment allowed me to plan, make decisions, and act, which in turn heightened my sense of peace.

This mindset—a commitment to living fully in the now—has liberated me from the weight of unnecessary regret. The past is immutable, but the present is an open door to infinite possibilities.

The lesson is clear: start over as often as necessary. Whether it's a minor frustration or a profound life challenge, remember that every moment holds the potential for transformation. Step forward and make the most of your time while you're alive.

Star Trek: Deep Space Nine

Star Trek: Deep Space Nine doesn't just build on the legacy of its predecessors—it boldly charts its course, delivering lessons that resonate far beyond the stars. Among its most profound teachings is its exploration of the past: how it shapes us, how we perceive it, and how we can ultimately reclaim power over it.

This lesson is perfectly embodied in the Changelings, a species of shapeshifters, and their most iconic member, Odo, the Chief of Security aboard *Deep Space Nine*. Odo is defined by his ability to transform into virtually anything—a chair, a puddle of liquid, or even a piece of wall art—to solve crimes and maintain order. His shapeshifting ability, though practical in his role, is a powerful metaphor for how we engage with our memories.

Like Odo, the past is not set in stone. It is a fluid, constantly changing form depending on the lens through which we choose—or are forced—to view it. While Odo has meticulous control over his transformations, our memories are more slippery. They are shaped by emotions, moods, and mental states that distort their meaning, often without us even realizing it.

The past can feel light, manageable, and joyful when we are content. However, in moments of regret, fear, or sadness, those memories can become heavy and overwhelming, their weight magnified by our current emotional state. Deep Space Nine teaches us that the past is never as straightforward as it seems. Like Changelings, it can shift and reshape itself, influenced by forces we don't always see.

Recognizing the malleable nature of memory is liberating. We don't have to remain prisoners of past mistakes or painful experiences. The past doesn't define us; it evolves as we do. By shifting our perspective on how we interpret it, we reclaim our role as storytellers of our own lives.

The show reminds us to approach the past with caution and curiosity. Memories are less like static and unchanging photographs and more like weather patterns, dynamic and constantly in flux. This understanding allows us to step out of the emotional loops we often create, where unresolved moments of regret or failure replay in our minds, fueling self-doubt.

But *Deep Space Nine* takes this lesson further, connecting it to our emotional and physical well-being. Earlier *Star Trek* series often showed how clinging to the past could disrupt the characters' balance, leaving them emotionally frayed. *Deep Space Nine*, however, reframes the past as a tool for growth. It encourages us to see the fluidity of memory not as a threat but as an opportunity to reinterpret and heal.

This insight is deeply tied to our nervous system, which is highly sensitive to unresolved stress or lingering emotional pain. When we cling to painful memories or replay them without perspective, we keep our nervous system in a heightened state of arousal, like a pot boiling on a stove. But when we ground ourselves in the present and approach the past with compassion, we allow the nervous system to recalibrate, restoring emotional equilibrium and inner peace.

Science fiction has always reflected humanity's mirror, and *Deep Space Nine* is no exception. It reminds us that our memories—like Changelings—are not static truths. They are dynamic, complex, and shaped by countless variables. By accepting this, we free ourselves from regret and find balance and stillness.

Ultimately, *Deep Space Nine* offers more than just science fiction entertainment. It delivers a powerful message: We are not at the mercy of our past. We are its storytellers. And in the ever-changing dance between memory and meaning, we hold the pen.

The Reality Test

Certain events in our past undeniably occurred. These moments leave tangible marks on our lives, like driving into a pole and causing a bridge to collapse. Such events cannot be denied, just as there are moments in your life that remain objectively real. Yet, over time, if these memories continue to haunt you, it is not the events that cause discomfort, but the narratives you have created around them.

Your feelings about these events are shaped more by your internal dialogue than by the events themselves. Revisiting painful memories often involves reevaluating your interpretation, rather than the raw facts. This distinction is crucial: your stories about the past can either harm or heal you. By understanding this, you can begin to rewrite those narratives in a way that supports your growth and well-being.

Another perspective worth exploring is the notion of the past as an illusion. This doesn't mean dismissing lived experiences; it challenges our thinking. The reality test enables us to distinguish between what is real and what is made-up.

Try this exercise to see what's real and an illusion: Look around and identify the chair you are sitting in. Touch it and feel its surface. Measure its dimensions, weigh it, and note its color. Is it made of cloth, leather, or wood? When you interact with the chair, you can confirm its physical reality.

Conversely, attempt the same with a memory. Choose a particularly stressful experience and try to measure or touch it. You will find that while memories feel real, they are intangible and exist solely in your mind, shaped by imagination and perspective. Realizing this makes it easier to release their grip on your present.

Reframing Negative Memories

To take control of how the past influences you, consider this exercise: identify four memories that evoke strong negative emotions. Write them down in the spaces provided below or on a separate sheet of paper. Reflect on how these memories make you feel and the narratives you have constructed around them.

Your Memories:

1. _______________________________

2. _______________________________

3. _______________________________

4. _______________________________

This exercise is not about reliving painful experiences but about gaining clarity. Acknowledging these memories allows you to see them as stories rather than immutable truths. With this shift in perspective, you can reframe them in ways that empower you and bring peace to your present.

The fictionalized Changelings remind us that transformation is possible and inevitable. Memories, like shapeshifters, are fluid and ever-changing. By recognizing this, you gain the power to reshape your relationship with the past, turning it into a source of insight and growth rather than a weight that holds you back.

Breaking Free from Self-Limiting Beliefs

When we remain trapped by our past, it's often because we hold beliefs like:

- This shouldn't have happened to me.
- I made an unforgivable mistake.
- I'm the only one who would do something like this.
- Something is inherently wrong with me.

To challenge these beliefs, ask yourself:

- What makes me so unique that I should be exempt from life's challenges?
- Has anyone else in human history had a similar experience?
- How have my "mistakes" shaped who I am today?
- What strengths or wisdom have I gained from these experiences?

Your power lies not in rewriting the past but in how you interpret and use it. Like The Doctor from *Star Trek: Voyager*, embracing the idea that "Here begins a new life" can be liberating, filling you with hope and optimism. Similarly, as Picard embraces his authentic journey, he frees himself from the distress of past regrets. Like Spock, recognizing that the past is gone allows you to be in the present moment. In this way, your interpretation of the past can set you free.

It's important to note that this isn't about denying reality or pretending that adverse events never happened. Instead, you're invited to release the interpretations that no longer serve you and to embrace the wisdom that your experiences have brought. For instance, if you made a mistake at work, instead of dwelling on failure, reinterpret it as a learning opportunity. Every moment, even those you deem mistakes, has shaped you and given unique insights and strengths. Use them to build a meaningful present and future, starting right now.

Reality is undeniable, but how we interpret it shapes our experience. Imagine you're driving and accidentally hit a pole, causing damage. The event is actual—there's physical evidence, documentation, and perhaps even witnesses. But years later, if this memory still causes you distress, it's not the event that troubles you. It's the story you've created around it: perhaps you've labeled yourself as careless or unworthy. It's these interpretations, and not the event that makes you suffer.

Much like the weather, the past is unpredictable and ever-changing in your mind; simply understanding that shift will allow you to hold your memories more lightly and prevent them from casting shadows over your present. Remember, the story you tell yourself about your past is not fixed—it's a continuous process of being rewritten through the lens of your current perspective, empowering you to take control of your narrative.

Your task isn't to "perfect" your past or "erase" all regrets. That's impossible. Instead, understand that your memories are malleable interpretations, not fixed truths. This understanding can free you to engage fully with the present moment and move confidently toward your future goals.

To move forward, take small, meaningful steps to live authentically and align your actions with your values. Focus on what you can do rather than being stuck in what might have been. Like every *Star Trek* character we've discussed, you hold the power to choose how to view your past and how to move forward from here, instilling a sense of determination and proactivity in you.

Worksheet

List four events that you consider to be your significant past errors. Don't judge or explain—acknowledge them:

1. _______________________________
2. _______________________________
3. _______________________________
4. _______________________________

After completing this list, reflect on each item through these lenses:

- What did this experience teach me?
- How did it shape who I am today?
- What strengths or insights did I gain from this challenge?

Living in the Present

Consider these truths:
- The past exists only in your mind.
- Your interpretations of events, not the events themselves, cause suffering.
- Your "mistakes" have helped shape your character and wisdom.
- You can choose new meanings for old events.

- Your power always lies in the present moment.

Write about what these truths mean to you: __

____

____

____

____

Recognize the Shapeshifter: When revisiting past events, remember that your current emotional state influences how you perceive them. Ask yourself, "How might I view this memory differently if I were in a better mood?"

Write about what this means to you: _______________

____

____

____

____

Seek Perspective: Before letting a past decision weigh heavily on you, discuss it with trusted friends or mentors. They can often provide valuable context and help you see situations more objectively.

Write about what this means to you: __________

____

____

____

____

Practice present-moment awareness: _________

When you dwell on the past, gently redirect your attention to the present moment. What opportunities are currently available to you?

Write about what this means to you: __________

____

____

____

____

Use Your Experience Wisely: Instead of viewing past decisions as mistakes, treat them as data points that inform your future choices. What lessons can you extract without carrying the emotional burden?

Write about what this means to you: ________

____

____

____

____

In conclusion, take a moment to reflect: Have you ever honestly asked yourself whether the life you envisioned for yourself would've brought you the peace or joy you seek? It's easy to get caught up in the fantasy of "what could have been," but living in that shadow is not the path meant for you.

Even those who achieved remarkable feats, like President John F. Kennedy, who guided a nation but was tragically taken from us at the young age of 46, or Dr. Martin Luther King Jr., who won the Nobel Peace Prize and inspired millions, yet was taken from the world at just 39, were not immune to hardship and loss. They, too, faced their battles, reminding us that life is unpredictable and often fleeting.

Rather than getting lost in comparisons or the allure of what could have been or should have been, shift your focus to your current life. Embrace the present and take small, purposeful actions to live authentically, aligning your daily choices with your core values. By embracing the present, you may evolve to appreciate the life you have because it's the only life you have.

Reflect on the many blessings in your life and let them serve as a foundation for building a meaningful and fulfilling future. You can shape your reality, one choice at a time. Your true strength lies in the present moment. Begin living intentionally today, for it is in the quality of your choices that the future is crafted. Don't wait for a tomorrow that may never come—start creating the life you want now.

Chapter 4

The Power of Choice

Nothing is more difficult, and therefore more precious, than to be able to decide. Napoleon Bonaparte

Early one morning, I awoke with an inspired thought: *The quality of my life depends on my choices.* This simple yet profound realization struck me deeply. Choice is a fundamental principle of human existence, yet it is often underestimated or ignored. Does this idea resonate with you? It did with me as I reflected on it that morning. I realized that people do not always make the best decisions for themselves. If we are guilty of anything, we often fail to exercise our power of choice thoughtfully.

However, this realization is not a cause for despair but an opportunity for continual growth and improvement. Recognizing the power of choice can illuminate a new path forward, revealing principles that guide better decision-making and greater self-awareness. Life teaches us the consequences of underestimating our ability to choose, decide, and act. When

I began to see that choice is a true superpower, certain principles came to mind:

- *The Power of a Clear Mind*: Good decisions are made with mental clarity. This means avoiding impulsive decisions when intoxicated by excitement or clouded by a low mood. Decisions made in a balanced mind are more likely to align with your true intentions.

- *The Power of Seeking Advice*: Getting advice from informed people can be valuable, but it can often serve as a cautionary light, urging you to pause. Feeling uncertain signals you to slow down, gather more information, and wait until you are confident in your direction.

- *The Power of a Mastermind*: Throughout history, leaders have relied on the collective wisdom of a mastermind. Engaging with others for thoughtful discussion can provide clarity and fresh perspectives, making it a powerful tool in the decision-making process.

- *The Power of a Firm Decision*: When emotions run high, it is easy to feel insecure and indecisive. A firm decision can steady your mind and provide a sense of resolve and peace.

These principles form the foundation for gaining clarity and greater confidence as you navigate life. By embracing your ability to choose, you will uncover valuable insights about past decisions, learn from them, and use this knowledge to guide your future. This awareness will not only enlighten you but also increase your self-assurance. Let's explore these superpowers individually.

Embracing the Power of Choice

No one sets out to make poor decisions. Understanding this can foster compassion for yourself when you falter. Life is a continuous learning journey, offering lessons through every experience. When viewed in this light, life becomes a schoolroom, and every decision— good or bad—serves as a step toward growth.

Recognizing that you always have the power of choice, even in challenging situations, is vital. Often, emotional distress leads us to think that others are better equipped to make decisions for us. While others may offer insights or expertise, no one is better suited to make decisions for you than *you*. Trusting yourself is one of life's most empowering realizations.

Moreover, saying *no* is a crucial aspect of making choices. Saying *no* halts external pressures and gives you the time and space to gather information and decide on your terms. Even in moments of doubt or distress, you can pause, reflect, and take control of the situation.

In her electronic newsletter, *Does It Matter*, Dr. Eleanor Hooks wrote an article titled "Saying 'Yes' Too Quickly." The article explores how some people struggle with saying *no*. Hooks notes that saying "no" comes more naturally in some cultures. For example, in Argentina, the Spanish word *mañana* often implies "not today" rather than a specific future time. There are multiple ways to say *no* in Japan, including the word *iie* (pronounced *ee-ay*). In Nigerian Pidgin, *no* is expressed as "I'm not doing that."

Saying *yes* too quickly can lead to problems, often leaving people struggling to say *no* later. Hooks advocates for practicing a "slow yes," emphasizing that many of life's troubles may stem from saying *yes* too hastily and failing to say *no* soon enough. Slowing down and allowing our nervous system to process events before making decisions is crucial.

Thus, a "slow yes" and a "quick no" can prevent unnecessary stress and regret. After all, once you have more information or feel fully aligned with a request, statement, or decision, you can always change your mind and say *yes* later. I have developed a simple exercise to help you internalize the power of saying *no*. I will ask you two questions and invite you to answer with a straightforward *yes* or *no*.

There is no need to explain your answer. The goal is to remind you that, regardless of the circumstances, you always have the power to decide. By practicing this exercise and reflecting on the principle of choice, you will come to appreciate that every decision—big or small—shapes the quality of your life. Recognizing this power is the first step toward greater freedom, clarity, and self-awareness. Choose wisely, and you will thrive. Here are two questions to help you experience the power of an honest *yes* or *no*:

- Do you want to buy a rusty truck from a salvage yard that doesn't have a motor, even though you're not in the business of repairing old vehicles? Yes or No (circle one)
- Do you want to move away from Georgia and quit a job you love to move to Alaska to be with someone you just met? Yes or No (circle one)

If you complete this simple exercise in integrity, you have proven that you can say *no*. Your ability to give an authentic *no* is a superpower, so use it.

Of course, there are always outliers—the people on the fringe—but most people who are not into antique trucks would not buy one. It is also possible for someone to be swept off their feet, throw caution to the wind, and move to Alaska on the spot with a stranger. However, most people would not do it, and you would probably say *no* if a stranger asked you to move. Remember, the ability to say *no* is a powerful tool, a silver bullet that keeps you in control and safe when you are pressed to decide before you are ready.

Reflection Exercise

How did you feel when you declined the scenarios above? Free write your response: ______

____

____

____

____

Did you notice that if you had said yes to either of the scenarios, it could have changed your life and produced results that may not have been in your best interest? Free write your response:

____

____

____

____

Were you surprised by your choices, and do you see how saying yes or no could lead to unexpected results? Free write your response:

____

____

____

____

Owning Your Decisions

Checking in with yourself and making decisions based on your values is not just essential but transformative. When you give an honest *yes* or *no,* you exercise control over your life and empower yourself to live authentically. This self-assured decision-making allows you to accept the results with clarity and confidence.

You can always take responsibility for your future regardless of your past choices. Decision-making is a skill; and, like any skill, it improves with practice. By grounding your preferences in your values, you establish a reliable framework to guide you, even during times of emotional distress or external pressure.

When you surrender your *power of choice* to others, you forfeit your inherent agency—the ability to steer your life in the direction you desire. However, when you make deliberate choices, you protect your well-being and align your life with your authentic self.

This intentionality fosters a sense of contentment and acceptance because, regardless of the outcome, you know the decision was yours. Conversely, allowing your decisions to be dictated by anxiety, confusion, or overwhelm can leave you feeling like a leaf swept away by the wind—disconnected, adrift, powerless, and disillusioned.

Moreover, believing you are merely a follower, incapable of making your own choices, can leave a sour taste in your mouth long after the moment has passed. This mental loop of regret and self-doubt can be suffocating, like vultures circling over unresolved feelings. However, there is an antidote: remind yourself that you made the best decision possible with the information you had at the time. This realization is profoundly freeing. It liberates you from the weight of the opinions of others and the burden of hindsight, affirming that you acted with integrity given the circumstances.

Moreover, exercising the power of choice does more than build confidence; it restores your sense of control and self-respect. Every decision made from a place of authenticity strengthens your ability to trust yourself, creating a positive cycle of empowerment. Over time, this practice reshapes how you and others perceive yourself. You step into the world with the poise of someone who knows they are in the driver's seat of their own life.

There is no better way to grow and feel empowered than by fully embracing your ability to choose. With each deliberate and heartfelt *yes* or *no*, you become the master of your destiny, the captain of your soul. Start today and watch how boldly owning your decisions transforms your life.

Free Write Exercise

What does the power of choice mean to you?

____

____

____

____

Reflection: How can exercising this power help you make better choices in your life? _________

____

____

A clear mind is essential when exercising the power of choice. Stress will cloud your judgment and impair your ability to think clearly. If you are overwhelmed, it is not the right time to make significant decisions. Waiting for mental clarity allows you to approach choices with greater focus and wisdom.

Governments, especially those in the West, recognize the importance of clear thinking in decision-making. In the United States, minors cannot enter into contracts or make life-altering decisions like marriage or military enlistment without a guardian's approval. This safeguard acknowledges that immaturity and lack of mental clarity can lead to poor choices.

Similarly, notaries are instructed to ensure signers of legal documents understand what they are doing. The notary may refuse to proceed if someone appears confused or under the influence. Civil law further protects individuals from binding agreements made while intoxicated, underscoring the necessity of a sober and clear mind.

Most assuredly, a foggy mind affects all areas of life, from speech and recall to physical performance. In my own experience, mental clarity has been pivotal. During my Taekwondo training, I performed at my best when I was focused and calm. On one occasion, when stress clouded my mind, it was evident in my sparring, making my movements awkward and stiff. My *sensei* noticed, though he didn't know the cause of my poor performance.

A similar situation occurred in graduate school when a professor observed that my writing lacked fluency. He pointed out that emotional distress was blocking my creative flow, and he was right. Whether driving, speaking, or making decisions, a clear mind makes all the difference.

Spiritual facilitator Cindy Teevens puts it aptly: when you are in a "stupid state," your mind is clouded, and this fog can impact every aspect of your life. Teachers, for example, recognize that students evaluate courses more fairly when in a positive emotional state. A low grade can result in a skewed evaluation due to stress, while a joyful classroom discussion often leads to a more balanced assessment. The same principle applies to your decisions—positive emotions and mental clarity enhance your judgment.

Moreover, clear thinking requires sobriety. While we often associate intoxication with substances, emotional intoxication, especially in romantic relationships, can be equally impairing. The euphoric "in love" phase, as described by Gary Chapman in *The 5 Love Languages: The Secret to Love that Lasts*, can obscure reality.

Decisions made during this phase may not be rational because they are driven by intoxicating emotions rather than clear-headed judgment. Rushing into commitments, such as marriage, under the influence of a romantic high can lead to unconscious decisions that result in regret. Taking time to let emotions settle allows for more thoughtful choices.

The Motown group, the Supremes, offered timeless advice in their 1965 hit: "Stop! In the name of love, before you break my heart." Considering and reflecting is a wise approach, whether in romance or any other significant decision. Remember, the power of a clear mind is your greatest ally in making choices that lead to lasting success and happiness.

Free Write Exercise

What does the power of a clear mind mean to you? _______________________________________

____

____

____

____

Reflection

How can exercising the power of a clear mind help you make better choices in your life? ______

____

____

____

____

We all need help sometimes, and seeking assistance is crucial when in emotional distress. The power of seeking advice lies in acknowledging this truth: when you need help, getting the proper support is essential. During times of emotional turmoil, we often turn to people we trust—family, friends, or spiritual advisors, such as pastors or mentors. These are trusted individuals who hold positions of influence for a reason, but it is vital to approach such moments with care and discernment.

When you are hurting, sharing your deepest emotions with someone is akin to opening your soul. However, not everyone is equipped to handle the weight of your pain. As the New Testament warns, *Do not throw your pearls to pigs; if you do, they may trample them under their feet and turn and tear you to pieces.*

This caution is not about labeling others as bad but understanding human limitations. Even well-meaning people may struggle to hold space for your stressful emotions because we are all shaped by our experiences and emotional bandwidth.

Indeed, if you find someone who listens with respect, empathy, and care, cherish that relationship. These individuals, whether family, friends, or spiritual advisors, can be invaluable allies, providing the support you need on your healing journey. Conversely, if you leave a conversation feeling worse, as though your vulnerability has been mishandled or misunderstood, it is a clear sign to step away.

Some people can only process what you share through the lens of their own stories and assumptions. In the words of Byron Katie, *they do not hear you; they hear their story*. This can lead to unintentional harm, as their advice may reflect their biases rather than meet your needs.

When I experienced clinical depression nearly five decades ago, mental health treatment was far less accessible, especially in the black community. In the 1970s, many people who were suffering emotionally were left to endure their psychological pain alone and in silence. Thankfully, we live in an era where mental health awareness has grown exponentially, and resources are more widely available.

Today, mental health professionals bring a wealth of knowledge and techniques to support those in need. While the demand for services is high, the options for finding a qualified therapist or counselor are abundant. From cognitive-behavioral techniques to mindfulness practices and beyond, therapists are equipped with a diverse toolkit to support your journey toward emotional well-being.

The ability to seek advice is crucial to making informed and healthy decisions. It can lead to healing and growth. The key is to seek it from the right sources and trust yourself to discern who can help you the most. Therapists and counselors often use specific therapeutic approaches to help individuals identify and address emotional and psychological challenges. Here are some widely recognized therapeutic techniques:

- *Cognitive Behavioral Therapy* (CBT): This approach helps clients identify and challenge distorted thoughts and beliefs contributing to negative emotions. Therapists work with clients to reframe these thoughts, replacing harmful thinking patterns with more constructive ones.

CBT emphasizes that our emotions often stem from how we interpret events rather than the events themselves. By pinpointing and addressing these distortions, clients can begin to feel better and make more balanced decisions.

- *Dialectical Behavior Therapy* (DBT): DBT incorporates mindfulness and emotion regulation techniques to help clients manage stress, enhance interpersonal skills, and develop self-acceptance. This therapy is especially effective for individuals struggling with intense emotions or relationship difficulties, fostering a greater sense of control and understanding.

- *Eye Movement Desensitization and Reprocessing* (EMDR): EMDR is particularly effective for individuals who have experienced trauma or suffer from post-traumatic stress disorder (PTSD).

This technique involves recalling distressing memories while engaging in guided eye movements or other bilateral stimulation, which can help the brain process and neutralize the emotional impact of the trauma.

- *Gestalt Therapy*: Gestalt focuses on the present moment and the connection between thoughts, feelings, and actions. Therapists encourage clients to take responsibility for their emotions and behaviors while helping them reframe stressful thoughts. This approach fosters self-awareness and empowers clients to take control of their actions and choices.

- *Exposure Therapy*: Exposure therapy is a systematic approach to treating anxiety, depression, PTSD, and phobias. Clients gradually confront their fears in a controlled and supportive environment, helping them become desensitized to triggers and reduce their emotional distress over time.

- *Somatic Experiencing* (SE): Developed by Dr. Peter A. Levine, this body-oriented therapeutic approach focuses on processing and releasing trauma stored in the body. SE addresses the physical sensations associated with trauma, promoting healing by helping clients reconnect with their bodily experiences and resolve lingering emotional or physical symptoms.

There are many more approaches to treating people in emotional distress. If you are hurting, seek help. However, there are still reasons for caution.

Exercise

List the challenges you face. Start your list here, but be exhaustive. Others will only see your work if you show it to them.

1. _______________   3. _______________
2. _______________   4. _______________
5. _______________   7. _______________
6. _______________   8. _______________

Choosing the Right Support

When searching for a therapist, it is essential to approach the process thoughtfully and carefully. Not every therapist will be a good fit for you, so finding one who aligns with your needs and values is vital. A competent therapist understands this and will agree that the therapeutic relationship must feel right for both parties. Look for a therapist who can see the best in you, even when you struggle to see it for yourself. Keep exploring options until you find someone who genuinely supports you as you navigate your emotional challenges.

Remember, choosing a therapist means opening your heart to another person; this is not a decision to be taken lightly. You are too precious to entrust yourself to someone unqualified or unsuitable for your needs. The right therapist can improve your life, while the wrong one may cause further harm. You'll know you've found the right match when you feel seen, heard, and understood during your conversations.

When I first faced emotional difficulties in the 1970s, I was barely 20 years old. At that time, I didn't even know that counselors or therapists existed. I turned to a family member who also had no awareness of mental health professionals. In an unexpected turn of events, he took me to a voodoo counselor who said I was cursed. It's amusing to reflect on that now, but I was overwhelmed by the emotional weight placed on me at the time.

My search for help continued, and I mistakenly believed I needed glasses, thinking my distress stemmed from poor vision. A kind optometrist prescribed glasses, though I later learned they were clear lenses that likely caused more harm than good.

Looking back, I wonder how different my life might have been if I had been aware of therapy and sought professional help. You don't have to endure psychological distress alone. Seeking professional help is a powerful step toward taking control of your mental health.

Choosing Carefully Within Religious Communities

Religious communities can provide comfort, but they can also be potential pitfalls when seeking guidance for emotional struggles. Ministers or spiritual leaders who claim to be connected to a Higher Power are often viewed as figures of authority and trust. If you are in emotional distress, it is natural to turn to them, hoping they have the answers you seek.

However, many ministers are not trained in mental health. While some are excellent counselors with proper credentials, others may only offer prayer, which may not fully address your needs. If a minister is not qualified to provide counseling, they should refer you to a mental health professional. Be cautious when entrusting your emotional well-being to someone untrained. Vulnerability during times of distress requires thoughtful, deliberate action. Choose a qualified therapist or counselor to provide the professional care you need.

I speak from experience. Early in my life, I trusted a minister with my struggles, but he was ill-equipped to support me. He offered prayer when I needed practical tools to navigate my emotional challenges. Although I was deeply engaged with the church then, the minister's limitations left me feeling unsupported. While I eventually found the strength to leave that church, the experience was a valuable lesson on the importance of making a good decision when seeking a mental health provider. I am not anti-clergy; I am simply urging you to approach such relationships with caution when addressing mental health concerns.

The rise of life coaches in the 21st century has produced various titles, including personal development, mindset, and transformation coach. While many excellent coaches can guide you effectively, it's essential to remember that anyone can call themselves a life coach or a variation of the title. Certification is not required, and standards can vary widely. If you are considering a coach, research their qualifications and ensure they align with your needs.

I have had mostly positive experiences with life coaches, but two encounters left me uneasy. After my divorce, I sought guidance from a coach who claimed to understand my situation. During our only meeting, I quickly realized he was not a good fit for me. He dismissed my feelings and implied I was entirely at fault for my circumstances. That moment taught me a valuable lesson: trust your instincts. If a coaching relationship doesn't feel right, walking away is okay.

Later, as I pursued becoming a life coach, I faced rejection from a coaching organization during the vetting process. The feedback was vague, and I was not allowed to improve. This experience reinforced the importance of clear communication and mutual respect in coaching relationships. While the organization may not have been a fit for me, it was a reminder to protect my mental health and seek relationships that foster growth.

Self-Awareness in Decision-Making

Whether you choose a therapist, a spiritual leader, or a life coach, the process requires self-awareness and discernment. A proper professional can guide you toward healing and growth, but the wrong one can hinder your progress or cause further harm. Take the time to carefully evaluate your options, trust your instincts, and never settle for less than what you truly need. Seeking advice and support is a powerful step in reclaiming control over your life, and making informed choices is one of the most empowering decisions you can make.

Exercise

List the therapists, pastors, and friends who helped or are helping you. In the second column, add how they made you feel. Do not hold back.

1. _____________ ___________________________
2. _____________ ___________________________
3. _____________ ___________________________
4. _____________ ___________________________

Choose Wisely

It's time to release the grip of regret and let go of choices that have left a bitter taste in your mouth. Those decisions served their purpose—they taught you valuable lessons. Now, you are equipped with the knowledge to make more informed decisions. Be grateful for the growth you have gained and the clarity you now possess. Embrace your ability to make informed choices and take action to secure the support you need.

Seeking advice and building a support network are powerful steps toward making sound decisions. However, it is essential to understand the roles of those in your life and use their strengths appropriately. For instance, while you may have a trained therapist in your family, they are unlikely to serve as your therapist. Why? Because therapy requires neutrality and professional boundaries, which are difficult to maintain in a family relationship.

A family therapist may refer you to a neutral professional, ensuring you have the space to speak freely without the complexities of family dynamics. Respect their expertise while keeping them in the family category—where they can still encourage and support you in other meaningful ways.

Trusted family members who are not therapists can also be invaluable. These individuals often provide emotional support in ways that feel immediate and personal. They may offer comfort and reassurance when you're struggling and need daily encouragement. You might even have one family member who stands by you like a stone wall, ready to lend an ear when needed; when your mind feels clouded or overwhelmed, having someone to talk to can make all the difference.

However, it's crucial to remember that these trusted family members are not replacements for professional therapy. They're part of your broader support network that might include friends, mentors, or spiritual advisors. Each plays a distinct role in your journey to making better choices and navigating life's challenges.

A sound support system helps you balance immediate needs with long-term healing. Therapists bring expertise, objectivity, and a structured approach to tackling deep-seated issues. Family members and friends offer emotional support and provide day-to-day companionship. This network empowers you to feel supported, grounded, and ready to make thoughtful decisions.

When you seek advice, you are not just asking for help but also taking control of your future. You are demonstrating courage and a willingness to grow. Surround yourself with people who uplift and inspire you, and do not be afraid to set boundaries where needed. Trust your instincts, lean on your support network, and choose the path that aligns with your values and goals. This is how you harness the power to make informed choices.

Exercise

Free Write: What does the power of seeking advice mean to you? ________________________

____

____

____

Reflection: How can exercising this power help you make better choices in your life? _________

____

____

____

The Power of a Mastermind

Making good decisions is one of the most vital life skills. Yet, it is easy to find ourselves overwhelmed, blinded by emotion, or stuck in a narrow perspective. This is where the *power of a mastermind* comes into play. A mastermind is an intentional gathering of people to help solve a problem, gain clarity, or make a significant decision. It's not about handing over your power to others but harnessing collective wisdom to make better-informed choices.

What is a Mastermind

At its core, a mastermind is a collaborative effort. It could involve two or more people pooling their knowledge, experience, and insights to help you achieve your goal. When used effectively, a mastermind can clarify, uncover your blind spots, and illuminate options you may not have considered. A well-chosen mastermind doesn't dictate your decision but instead supports you in seeing the bigger picture, ultimately enabling you to make the best choice for yourself.

Masterminds can be formed for nearly any purpose: starting a business, making a significant purchase, navigating life changes, or planning long-term goals. They are invaluable when decisions substantially affect finances, emotions, or time investments.

The following examples highlight how a mastermind could have transformed my decision-making processes in key moments of my life. From my example, you may be inspired to convene a mastermind when a crucial decision needs to be made.

The Boat Story

Buying a boat was not inherently bad because I could afford it. However, I didn't approach the decision with a clear mind. I was emotionally vulnerable and assumed that sellers had my best interests at heart. This flawed assumption and my lack of experience led to costly mistakes.

In hindsight, forming a mastermind would have been invaluable. Having a diverse team, including an experienced boater and a friend who understands my physical limitations, could have helped me make a sound decision. They would have highlighted critical factors, such as the practical challenges of boat ownership, particularly for individuals with physical disabilities. They might have guided me toward alternatives or helped me reconsider whether a boat fit my lifestyle and capabilities.

The result? I bought three boats in rapid succession. Each one had problems, and one did not have a working motor. I did not understand that sometimes sellers are liars, and I did not heed the ancient adage, *caveat emptor*—let the buyer beware. I could have saved myself money, time, and frustration when buying a boat. Instead, I learned a hard lesson: important decisions made in isolation often have avoidable consequences.

The Lawnmower Story

When my lawnmower broke, I faced the challenge: maintaining three acres of land. My initial solution? A small tractor. I was enamored with bush-hogging grass, even though I had no experience and no livestock to feed. Thankfully, I consulted a farmer with years of experience. Without hesitation, he steered me toward a zero-turn lawnmower. His reasoning was simple: a tractor was unnecessary and impractical for my needs. His expertise saved me from making an expensive mistake.

This informal mastermind made all the difference. His advice was grounded in hands-on experience, something I was missing.

Thanks to his guidance, I made one of the best decisions ever. The right mastermind can be a shortcut to wisdom, helping you navigate potential pitfalls and find smarter, more intelligent solutions.

The House Story

When I retired, I was eager to begin a new chapter of my life. I found the perfect home and purchased it almost entirely through virtual tours. The house was beautiful, with a stately façade and a charming porch that spanned its entire width. However, I overlooked one crucial detail: accessibility. Living with a physical disability, I could no longer manage the stairs easily; yet, the house had steps leading inside and to the second floor, where I had planned to set up my office.

In my excitement, I failed to consider how these stairs would impact my daily life, especially as I aged. It was not until I consulted a mastermind of physical therapists that I truly understood the gravity of my mistake. They vividly depicted the risks involved, such as falling down the stairs. Their professional insights helped me realize that the house, although beautiful, wasn't practical for me. With their guidance, I decided to sell and move into a more accessible home.

This experience reinforced a crucial lesson: emotions can cloud one's judgment. Thus, masterminds can bring objectivity to emotionally charged decisions and offer clarity when needed. Benefits include:

- *Gain Perspective*: A mastermind brings together diverse viewpoints, helping you see angles you might miss on your own.

- *Access Expertise*: By including individuals with relevant experience, you can make informed decisions based on knowledge, rather than guesswork.

- *Uncover Blind Spots*: Other individuals can identify weaknesses in your plan or assumptions you might not have questioned.

Masterminds can be formed for various decisions, such as choosing between universities, starting a business, or even buying a car. For instance, suppose you're considering a proprietary university with an appealing program but a high price tag. A mastermind could include graduates, financial advisors, and professors from public universities who can help you weigh the benefits against the potential debt incurred by enrolling in a for-profit institution.

Similarly, a mastermind might connect you with investors, industry experts, and marketing professionals if you launch a business. Their collective insights could refine your strategy, reduce risks, and lead you to success.

Remember, a mastermind does not take over your decision-making responsibility. Instead, it equips you with the tools and knowledge to make your best choice. Whether you are facing a minor question or a life-changing decision, the power of a mastermind can be transformative.

Ultimately, decision-making is a skill that can be learned. The best decision-makers often benefit from the collaboration that comes with a mastermind. When you engage the power of a mastermind, you create a framework for success that can save you time, money, and heartache. Do not underestimate the value of collective wisdom.

What does the power of a mastermind mean to you? _______________________________

____

____

____

Reflection: How can exercising this power help you make better choices in your life?

____

____

____

____

The Power of a Firm Decision

Making decisions can be daunting, especially for those navigating life while in emotional distress. However, mastering *the principle of a firm decision* is essential for stability and growth. When faced with choices, avoid falling into the trap of endless back-and-forth. Indecision breeds instability. As the scripture reminds us, *A double-minded individual is unstable in all his ways.* A firm decision can ground you, creating a sense of ease and direction. This inner peace is often a sign that you are on the right path.

However, if caught in a mental loop, it is a clear signal to pause. Instead of forcing a decision in uncertainty, step back and wait until clarity emerges. Premature decisions often lead to unnecessary complications, and while mistakes can sometimes be rectified, the process can be messy. It is better to pause and ensure your choice aligns with your values and long-term goals.

If you are called upon to decide now but remain unsure, here is what you should do: *say no.* Resist the urge or pressure to act hastily. Take time to reflect until you are sure of your path. Remember, you always have the power to choose—to say *no deal.*

The Ripple Effect of Good Choices

Making thoughtful choices will help you avoid unnecessary risks, maximize opportunities, and align your actions with your core values. As scripture advises, *Do not be anxious about anything.* Anxiety clouds judgment, but a clear mind will always foster better decision-making.

Leverage *the power of seeking advice* when your mind feels foggy. Guidance from trusted sources or a supportive mastermind group can provide valuable perspectives, especially when the stakes are high. Such a collaboration ensures you're not carrying the burden of significant decisions alone. Most assuredly, your choices will shape your life, often carrying long-lasting consequences. This is why the act of choosing wisely is so critical.

Once you have evaluated your options, sought counsel, and weighed potential outcomes, it is time to act decisively. Exercise *the power of a firm decision*, standing confidently and securely in your choice. Avoid wavering or second-guessing yourself, as this can undermine your resolve and damage your relationships. But decisions made with clarity and conviction foster trust, strengthen relationship bonds, and bolster self-confidence.

Remember, life is a journey of growth and learning. Not every decision will be perfect, but every conscious choice teaches valuable lessons for all. Be compassionate with yourself regardless of the outcome of your calculated decision. Combining thoughtful consideration, collaboration, and firm decisive action will create a more meaningful and fulfilling life for yourself, your family, and those around you.

To underscore the point, embrace the power of clarity in every decision and trust the process. When you make informed choices, you secure a brighter, more purposeful future.

Free Write Exercise

What does the power of a firm decision mean to you? _______________________________

____

____

____

____

Reflection: How can exercising this power help you make better choices in your life?

____

____

____

____

Chapter 5

The Inner Trial of the Mind

You did not prosecute me; you prosecuted the God in you. Dr. P.S. Jagadeesh Kumar

When I lived in emotional distress, I carried an unbearable burden of self-judgment. It was not intentional; I did not choose it. My mind seemed to run on autopilot, feeding me endless loops of limiting beliefs. I did not feel worthy, and my behavior reflected it. In that state, I convinced myself that others disliked me.

The cycle was relentless, like a never-ending storm of self-criticism that ceaselessly echoed in the chambers of my mind. There were moments of clarity because, deep down, the mind longs to free itself. However, those moments were fleeting as I went up and down, moving from hope to despair. These moments remind me of how a college classmate once described me: "The man who is sometimes up and sometimes down."

My default was so firmly set to self-loathing that positive thoughts could not stick. In many ways, I had become accustomed to thinking badly about myself. It felt normal, even though it was anything but "normal." When I was in graduate school in the early 1980s, I tried to capture how I felt in verse:

I've never been to Vietnam, But I've endured a war within—A silent war, invisible to all… A mind that turned on itself, Tortuous, relentless, unforgiving… Fighting to drag me into captivity.

While trapped in this mindset, life passed me by as I dwelled in insecurity. I turned down an opportunity to attend law school full-time for free at the university where I worked. I vividly remember lying on my bed for hours, absorbed in *Star Trek* reruns on TV, using it as an escape. Significant events, the kind that shook the world, barely registered with me.

Even the attempted assassination of President Ronald Reagan in 1981, the Challenger explosion in 1986, and the terrorist attacks on 9/11 seemed far away to me due to my internal storm. My reality was one of mere survival, rather than full engagement with life.

Believing that the people in my life were against me only deepened my sense of isolation and paranoia. I felt like I was always on trial, as though I had to defend my existence. You may also resonate with some of these feelings if you live a life of emotional despair.

It is common for individuals who struggle emotionally to turn inward while carrying the weight of their imagined accusations. However, remember, you are not alone in this fight. Many others, including myself, have walked this path and found a way out. You are cared for and understood, and hope for your healing exists.

The focus of this chapter is to confront your imaginary trial directly. We are not here to tiptoe around the issue; we are stepping into the ring with bare fists! Suppose you, like me, have felt as if you have walked *in the valley of the shadow of death*, enduring feelings of unworthiness, being misunderstood, and constantly being judged. In that case, this is your opportunity to purge those emotions once and for all. We will air it all out now, confronting the guilt, regrets, shame, and self-doubt you feel, detoxifying the polluted system that once held you captive. This confrontation is not a punishment but a liberation. It is the first step towards a life free from self-judgment and recrimination.

Understand this from the outset: a life of relentless self-criticism is not the path to healing. There is a better way. However, before you can move forward, you must clear the slate. This is your opportunity to shed light on the lies you have been telling yourself and carrying. If you are like me, you have been the accuser, the accused, and the judge. The goal is not to assign guilt, but to face the weight of these unfair accusations, boldly confront them, and finally let them go once they are exposed to the truth.

You will rewrite the script once you have purged yourself of the junk you carry. Then, you will install new software: a healthier, kinder way of thinking. However, for now, let us start with the first step: putting yourself on trial, as I did, and finally breaking free from the chains of self-judgment. This process is not about being a victim of your thoughts but taking control of your life. You are the one in charge of your narrative, and you have the power to change it.

Prosecute Yourself

The United States judiciary is rooted in an adversarial system designed to achieve justice. The prosecutor represents the state, and a defense attorney fights for the accused. This dynamic creates a battleground for justice, but in this make-believe trial, you are both the prosecutor and the defendant. You'll channel the spirit of hard-nosed prosecutors with a legal lineage filled with zealous advocates who will fight tooth and nail to win.

They see the adversarial judicial system in this light: the good and the bad. You are stepping into their shoes now, embodying their unyielding determination to win. Your mission focuses on securing a conviction against yourself, an individual burdened with a mind entrenched in limiting beliefs, notions of unworthiness, and fear.

Furthermore, the courtroom itself presents a hostile and unforgiving environment for defendants. A stern and uncompromising judge presides, with a reputation for agreeing with the prosecution. Objections from the defense are typically met with the swift sound of the gavel and a booming voice saying, *"Overruled!"*

The jury consists of an assembly of all your inner critics, drawn from the most conservative and unforgiving precincts of your psyche, predisposed to view you in the harshest light. The courtroom gallery is also an aspect of your personality, offering murmurings of disapproval. It is as though an entire community of "haters" surrounds you, determined to ensure your defeat.

As the determined prosecutor, you rise to present the charges against yourself. Moreover, as the defendant, you are accused of offenses and crimes against yourself and others. And the prosecutor quickly rattles off a litany of charges echoing the style of the American Declaration of Independence, listing a history of "injuries and usurpations" you allegedly committed. With each point, the prosecutor drives home a narrative of your guilt:

- The times you have failed others.

- The moments you have been selfish or unkind.
- The opportunities you squandered.
- The relationships you strained.
- The individuals harmed by your callousness.
- The times when you say the wrong things to others.
- The times when you did not keep a trust.

You build a case so airtight that even you, as the defendant, struggle to find your balance.

Why undertake such a brutal self-examination? Because too many of us live with what I call the GRS Syndrome: guilt, regret, and shame. These emotions swirl in our minds, corroding our sense of self-worth and feeding an endless loop of self-condemnation. If you are like most people struggling with emotional distress, you know this pattern all too well. It begins with guilt over something you have done, which morphs into regret for having done it. Ultimately, it devolves into shame, and the belief that one is inherently flawed or unworthy may take root. It is a relentless and vicious cycle, and for years, I was trapped in it.

As I mentioned in Chapter 1, negative bias is a natural human tendency—our inclination to give more weight to undesirable experiences, emotions, or mistakes than to positive ones. This bias has its roots in our evolutionary past when our ancestors needed to be hyper-alert to threats in their hostile environments to survive. While this heightened sensitivity once protected us, it often manifests as harsh self-criticism today.

When we make a mistake or fall short of our expectations, this negative bias amplifies the emotional fallout. Instead of recognizing the lessons or growth that can come from our experiences, we fixate on our perceived shortcomings. We dwell on what went wrong, replaying our failures in a loop while our successes and strengths fade into the background. This distorted perception only deepens the emotional toll, making it harder to see ourselves clearly or with compassion.

However, by understanding this natural tendency, we can begin to overcome it. We can shift our perspective and adopt a more balanced view of ourselves, acknowledging our imperfections and our potential for growth.

When we're in the thick of emotional distress, though, this shift can feel impossible. Strategies to escape the vicious cycle of self-loathing may seem out of reach. Neuropsychiatrist Dr. Abraham Low once taught about managing distressing thoughts, while writer Byron Katie emphasizes questioning the narratives we tell ourselves. Yet, in those moments of inner turmoil, we often default to putting ourselves on trial, bombarding ourselves with accusations and harsh judgments.

But what if this trial could serve a different purpose? Instead of using it for self-punishment, we can foster greater self-understanding and compassion. You can confront those accusations head-on by putting yourself on trial—on paper. You'll see that while some criticisms may contain a grain of truth, they are far from the whole picture. The process helps you dismantle the idea that you are a villain, replacing it with a more accurate narrative: you are human, flawed, but capable of growth and redemption.

So, let us begin these court proceedings. Build your case against yourself—lay out the accusations, the evidence, the self-doubt. But then, dismantle it with the truth of who you are. Challenge those harsh judgments and recognize the fullness of your humanity. As scripture says, *The truth shall make you free.* This process isn't about erasing your past mistakes but understanding them, learning from them, and freeing yourself from the weight they carry.

Let's move forward, not with a desire to condemn but to heal.

The Prosecutor's Case

Step 1: The Criticisms. *Write down the complaints or accusations your inner critic makes about you.*

- Example: I sent a harsh email to someone at work in response to an email they sent me.

Write down four *specific* things your inner critic accuses you of because of that act.

- Example: I'm sorry I responded to that person in that way. I must be a terrible person.

1. ____________________________________

2. _______________________________________

3. _______________________________________

4. _______________________________________

Step 2: The Accusations. *List the charges your mind brings against you because of how you handled the situation.* These are the moments, actions, or patterns that evoke feelings of guilt, regret, or shame. For example, the defendant:

- made a crude remark in the presence of someone being supervised, and the word seemed to have wounded them.

- has entered and ended several romantic relationships.

- allowed fear and "imposter syndrome" to stop him from attending law school for free.

- got a divorce that evoked confusion, guilt, and worry.

Because of these actions, the prosecution, your inner critic, brings the following charges against you:

- You are a person of poor character.

- You are not trustworthy.
- You are a runner, and when relationships become difficult, you flee.
- You care only about yourself.
- You are harsh in your dealings with others.

It's your turn to prosecute yourself. List the charges your mind brings against you.

1. _______________________________________
2. _______________________________________
3. _______________________________________
4. _______________________________________

Step 3: The Evidence. *For each charge, describe why you feel this way.* Make a note of what happened. How did it impact you or others? Be as factual and objective as possible. Remember, this isn't about blaming or condemning yourself endlessly but understanding the root of your feelings.

- Example: When my supervisor at work judged me and altered my team based on

a co-worker's opinion without first talking with me, I resigned from my admin-
istrative position.

It's your turn: What's the proof for the
charges against you? List as many facts that
may be against you.

1. _______________________________________
2. _______________________________________
3. _______________________________________
4. _______________________________________

Furthermore, as a prosecutor, I submit
that the defendant's entire life has been marked
by his constant self-recrimination. I ask the
court for its indulgence as I summarize some
of these points here for context because the defendant has expressed his limiting beliefs in
many ways. These are some of the core aspects
of how he mistreated himself when he was in
emotional distress, especially when suffering
from depression.

The self-criticism and self-recrimination
he often heaped on himself is proof of his guilt
for failing humanity. Here is a recap of some of
the ways he failed himself and others by innocently engaging in this self-punishing behavior:

Negative Self-Talk

- *Internalized Shame*: He frequently replays past mistakes and perceived failures and holds himself responsible for events beyond his control, leading to feelings of guilt, regret, shame, and inadequacy. His lived experience is marked by internal dialogues such as "I'm not good enough," "I always mess things up," or "I'm a failure."

- *Catastrophizing*: He interprets setbacks as catastrophes, reinforcing feelings of worthlessness or helplessness. He practices "all-or-nothing thinking," as Dr. David Burns says in his book *Feeling Great*. This way of thinking creates an environment where he expects the worst.

Avoidance and Isolation

- *Self-punishment Through Isolation*: He withdraws from friends, family, or activities he once enjoyed, seeing himself as underserving of connection or support. He believes others would be better off without him and that he isn't worthy of love or care.

- *Helplessness*: He often feels helpless, thinking he cannot control situations. This sense of powerlessness feeds his anxiety and makes him avoid social interactions, even when opportunities for them exist.

Perfectionism and Unrealistic Standards

- *Unachievable Expectations*: He holds himself and others to high, and often perfectionistic standards, believing that constant achievement and ideal performance are necessary for acceptance. When those expectations aren't met, he responds with harsh self-criticism and is equally critical of others.
- *Constant Self-Evaluation*: He measures his self-worth by unrealistic standards, feeling he can never achieve or be enough to measure up.

Internalized Criticism of Others

- *Projecting Self-Blame onto Others*: He bases his self-worth on how he believes others see him. He assumes others judge or criticize him unfairly, even when no evidence supports that belief.

Ruminating on Regret and Mistakes

- *Replaying Negative Experiences*: He ruminates on past failures, missed opportunities, and perceived wrongdoings. This endless cycle of self-recrimination prevents his healing and reinforces feelings of incompetence.

Imposter Syndrome

- *Feeling Like a Fraud*: He feels like he is not enough, even when someone praises him.
- *Fear of Being Exposed*: He fears that all his flaws and weaknesses are there for all to see!

These are some of the ways the defendant lived as a depressed soul, which warrants his conviction by a just society. In a way, due to emotional distress, he has prosecuted himself. If he was his own worst enemy and perpetuated a cycle of guilt, shame, isolation, and self-doubt, why should we protect him now? If he cannot treat himself with compassion and love nor steadfastly challenge these negative internal narratives, healing can never begin, and that's due to his failures as a human.

Therefore, the **PEOPLE**, on behalf of all the victims harmed by the **DEFENDANT**, mainly due to his poor judgment and discernment, appeal to this **COURT** and its **JURY** to hand down the just verdict of **GUILTY**. We **PLEAD** that he shall live in shame and disgrace for the rest of his natural life.

II. Defend Yourself

Only God can judge me... Only God can judge me now. Nobody else, nobody else. Tupac Shakur

Tupac Shakur, the legendary rapper and poet, once declared in a song, *Only God can judge me*. Indeed, some of the lyrics in the song are ripe with explicit language, but do not allow them to distract you from their profound message that no one else can rightly judge anyone. This statement resonates deeply in the moments when we become our harshest critics. It reminds us that only God has the authority to condemn anyone.

My critical mind accuses me of several alleged crimes, including poor judgment, missed opportunities, and actions that hurt others, which I cannot undo. As the prosecutor—my inner critic—relentlessly presented a list of arguments against me, many laced with the innumerable limiting beliefs and negative thoughts I once endured and determined to prove my guilt, I stand accused and, in my mind, judged unjustly by those who know me.

However, today, I am taking the stand in defense, determined not to let this prosecutor trample over my entire life of service.

Debunking the Prosecutor's Case

As William Shakespeare wrote in Othello after the tragic murder of Desdemona, "Twas I that did it," underscoring the importance of owning our mistakes. I, too, have made my share of errors, from minor mistakes to significant failures. Who among us hasn't made mistakes on this human journey? Perfection is an illusion for humanity! We all stumble because life is inherently messy for everyone, and no one navigates it without scars. It's in acknowledging our faults that we pave the way for growth, making it a critical step in our personal development.

Admittedly, my past is marked by many moments I am not proud of, particularly in my marriages and other romantic relationships. I entered and ended relationships without considering the impact my decisions would have on others. My divorce, for instance, hurt not only my wife at the time and our children but also extended to my in-laws and acquaintances, whose feelings I failed to consider. These choices left me questioning my integrity.

Additionally, I made mistakes at work when I believed I was defending myself and spoke harshly to others. The weight of these missteps—both in my personal and professional life—has left me struggling with feelings of depression and confusion. I have devoted a significant part of my life to believing I am worthy of redemption, determined to learn from these experiences and seek further personal growth.

Furthermore, these mistakes are not the sum of who I am. I have reflected deeply on my errors, and as far as possible, I have sought forgiveness from others and myself. I have spent sleepless nights ruminating over the harm I might have caused others, feeling pain far more significant than anyone could have imposed upon me. This is not because I am a terrible person; it is because I care deeply about other people, perhaps too deeply.

The Scars of Sensitivity

Many of us who endure emotional pain share a common thread: a deep sensitivity to the feelings of others. This sensitivity, often perceived as a burden, is a profound gift. It enables us to connect deeply with those around us, understanding their joys and struggles in ways others might overlook.

Yet, this same gift can weigh heavily on us. It magnifies the sting of failure, the judgments of others, and the impossibly high standards we hold ourselves to. In our constant striving to be good, to make the right choices, and to please those around us, we can lose sight of the most valuable part of ourselves: our humanity.

The emotional wounds I've carried, which never fully healed, have shaped the person I am today. Despite the pain, I've achieved much in life: academic and professional successes, creative contributions that I'm proud of, and moments of meaningful connection with others. And yet, I often wonder how much more I could have accomplished had I been in a healthier state of mind.

At the same time, I've come to realize that these scars are not just reminders of what I've endured. They are also my teachers. They have shown me the path to healing, taught me the value of empathy, and illuminated what is possible when we refuse to give up on our dreams. My emotional pain, while challenging, has ultimately been a source of strength, guiding me to understand not just others but myself.

Feelings Are Not Facts

During the 1990s, I participated in a self-help group called Recovery, which was organized by Dr. Abraham Low and his patients in the mid-1900s. Dr. Low developed a technique called the Recovery Method. He reported that patients frequently found themselves in a "vicious cycle," a self-reinforcing loop of symptoms and reactions that exacerbated their suffering.

Here is one profound truth Dr. Low taught his patients: your thoughts and feelings, as persuasive as they may seem, are not the ultimate reality of who you are. He declared: "Feelings are not facts." They can lie to you, deceive you, and paint a distorted picture of danger, failure, or rejection that does not exist. They are like storm clouds that can temporarily obscure the sun and are fleeting if we learn to see through them. Our group was facilitated by a Recovery volunteer, who guided us through the Recovery Method to help us break the vicious cycle in the mind. The Method broadened our understanding of:

- *Symptoms and Fear:* Patients may experience symptoms such as anxiety, depression, or physical sensations like heart palpitations and night sweats. These symptoms often evoke fear, which amplifies their intensity, forming a vicious cycle.

- *Fear of the Fear:* The fear of experiencing these symptoms again creates a heightened sensitivity to any signs of their recurrence. This "fear of the fear" becomes a trigger, perpetuating a constant state of vigilance and anxiety.

- *Reactivity and Misinterpretation:* Patients frequently misinterpret normal or benign bodily sensations as signs of severe illness or danger, leading to overreactions. This reactive behavior intensifies their distress and further entrenches them in the cycle.

Dr. Low helped his patients *normalize* their lives in many ways, as Theresa taught us in Chapter 1. Theresa did not know Dr. Low, but she understood the universal truth he taught his patients. Dr. Low was famous for saying patients believed they were exceptional but feared they were only average. He emphasized that breaking the vicious cycle was possible, and he developed a technique that included the principles of self-awareness and self-control, which are central to the Recovery Method. His key strategies include:

- *Spotting*: Identifying and labeling the negative thoughts, feelings, and reactions that fuel the cycle.

- *Self-Endorsement*: Praising oneself for small steps toward self-control and emotional regulation.

- *Objectivity*: Encouraging patients to terminate anxiety by interpreting their symptoms and experiences in a calm, rational way rather than catastrophizing them.

- *Practice*: Repeatedly using these tools in everyday situations to build resilience and break free from the cycle.

Dr. Low's Recovery Method provides practical tools to reduce emotional overreaction to perceived character attacks, helps us gain perspective, fosters greater emotional stability, and enables patients to break the vicious cycle of emotional distress.

Many of us react to negative feelings with childish emotions, and we, like children, sometimes behave as if "a monster is under the bed" when none is there. Thus, we often shrink from and suppress negative emotions, internalizing them as part of our identity. In doing so, we create a foundation for our limiting beliefs to harden. However, today, this behavior ends. Today, we place these fears, doubts, and insecurities in the spotlight of this imaginary courtroom. We put them on trial, not to destroy ourselves but to expose these emotions for what they are—the untruths that have imprisoned us for far too long.

Put Your Limiting Beliefs on Paper

Jotting down your limiting beliefs can provide a sanctuary for being radically honest. You will list your "charges" against yourself, not for public consumption but for your liberation.

I will share some of the charges I once held against myself as examples, though I will keep the most personal ones to myself, as I advise you to do. You do not have to reveal your deepest vulnerabilities to anyone unless it helps them grow. What matters is that you face these charges head-on, confronting the guilt, regret, and shame that have haunted you.

In 2008, I had the pleasure of participating in Byron Katie's School for the Work, held in Los Angeles. Katie teaches students to put their thoughts on paper, a strategy she calls *The Work*, which allows them to identify and question their stressful beliefs. Writing down your thoughts slows the mind, often bringing unconscious beliefs into conscious awareness where they can be examined rationally. Doing *The Work* may help you create distance between you and your thoughts, making it easier to question them and discover new perspectives.

Katie's process, *The Work*, consists of four questions and the clincher, which she calls the *Turnaround*. These questions and the turnaround are designed to help you examine and challenge stressful thoughts:

- Is it true?
- Can you absolutely know that it's true?

- How do you react… what happens… when you believe that thought?
- Who would you be without the thought?

The Work challenges practitioners to answer the questions on paper—to put their minds on paper. Katie would say, "If you're going to fight a war, it's better to do it on paper." Once you've answered these questions, Katie invites you to consider *The Turnaround*. In The Work, you find "turnaround" thoughts true or truer than your initial thoughts. This involves searching for ways to counter your initial thoughts with opposing ones. Here's an example:

- Original Thought: They don't respect me.
- Turnaround: I don't respect myself.

However, finding *The Turnaround* in *The Work* is not enough. You are invited to find specific examples illustrating how these principles may be true, promoting deeper insight and self-awareness.

As I outlined, Dr. David Burns, a psychiatrist, teaches cognitive behavioral therapy (CBT) techniques to help individuals challenge and confront negative thoughts. Here are four ways he does so:

1. *Identify the Cognitive (Mental) Distortions*: Recognize distorted thinking patterns, such as catastrophizing, all-or-nothing thinking, or mind-reading, that contribute to negative emotions.
2. *Examine the Evidence*: Treat negative though-ts like hypotheses and challenge them by examining factual evidence for and against them, much like a scientist testing a theory.
3. *Reframe Thoughts*: Replace distorted or overly negative thoughts with balanced, realistic alternatives that better reflect the situation.
4. *Behavioral Experiments*: Test the validity of negative beliefs through actions or experiments, such as facing feared situations to gather real-world evidence against irrational fears.

These techniques are designed to help promote greater self-awareness and empower you to regain control over your emotional responses. Until you learn the strategies to help yourself, you'll likely behave like I do, both as prosecutor and defendant in a trial against yourself.

The Case for Forgiveness

Forgiveness is the cornerstone of humanity, a divine gift that liberates all human beings from the shackles of guilt and shame. The Bible offers countless reminders of this truth. Ephesians 4:32 urges us to be kind to one another, tenderhearted, and forgiving one another, as God in Christ forgave you. In *Matthew* 18:22, when Peter asked Christ how many times one should forgive, Jesus responded, not seven times, but seventy-seven times seven. Of course, by doing the math, Jesus did not mean to forgive only 490 times; He made the point that forgiveness is boundless.

It is possible that the Supreme Creator, God, expects humans to err and forgive themselves and others. Why should I, or anyone, hold myself to a higher standard? Life is not about avoiding mistakes; it is about learning from them. Each error is an opportunity for growth, a step toward becoming the person we are meant to be. Learning from our mistakes empowers us to shape our narratives and grow from our experiences.

Stories of Resilience

Angelo Caerlang

Angelo Caerlang, the celebrated Filipino writer of motivational and reflective essays on personal growth, published "A Reminder for You When You've Made So Many Mistakes in Life" for *Thought Catalog*, an online platform. Caerlang captures the sentiment expressed in the title beautifully, writing, "It's okay to fail, to mess up, and to feel horrible. You tried to figure it out, make the right call, and make the best decision possible. You're here to learn, and the lessons that came into your life were meant for you."

Furthermore, he offers a heartfelt reminder that mistakes are not permanent marks of failure but a bridge for greater growth and understanding. Caerlang's words reflect a profound empathy for those struggling with self-doubt and regret, assuring them that even missteps carry value.

Moreover, Caerlang's writings remind us of our capacity for self-discovery. He draws deeply from his own life experiences of hardship and failure. His candid storytelling resonates with readers who seek solace and encouragement in the face of adversity. Through his work, he empowers us to embrace our imperfections and view challenges as opportunities for personal growth and transformation.

His essay is a testament to his ability to connect with readers on a deeply emotional level, offering them hope and a renewed sense of purpose in their journeys. We can glean the following strategies from his writings when we feel we have made mistakes that cause emotional pain:

1. *Practice Self-Forgiveness*: Accept your imperfections and forgive yourself for past errors, recognizing that everyone makes mistakes as part of life's journey.

2. *Embrace Growth*: View mistakes as opportunities for learning and self-im-
provement, using them to grow in wisdom.
3. *Focus on the Present*: Avoid dwelling on
past mistakes by concentrating on the
present moment and taking actionable
steps to move forward.
4. *Maintain Hope*: Believe in your capacity
for redemption and trust that your mistakes do not define your worth or potential for a better future.

Caerlang's insights encourage us to perse-
vere despite setbacks, practice self-compassion,
and remain patient on our life's journey.

Jane Kristen Marczewski

Jane Kristen Marczewski, also known as
Nightbirde, was an American songwriter and
performer whose journey deeply resonates
with those facing emotional distress. She rose
to fame on *America's Got Talent* in 2021, where
her gift as a performer and her courage shone
as she shared her unrelenting battle with cancer

and the physical pain it caused, all while radiating hope, grace, and strength.

One of Nightbirde's original songs, "It's Okay," has become a global anthem, reminding us that stumbling and making mistakes are not failures, but a normal part of life. Her declaration, "I'm much more than the bad things that happened to me," highlighted the profound truth that our identities are shaped not by our struggles but by how we choose to heal and move forward.

Her story teaches us that life's uncertainties and hardships, though challenging, do not diminish our worth. Instead, they can refine us, fostering strength, compassion, and a deeper appreciation for beauty amid pain. Her courage and authenticity reflect the universal truth: life is messy but offers many opportunities for personal growth.

In moments of emotional distress, let Nightbirde's story inspire you to rewrite your narrative, embrace your journey, and understand that where you are now is just a chapter, not your entire story. Her experience facing cancer suggests these strategies for handling challenges:

1. *Radical Acceptance*: She embraced life as it was, even when it felt unfair.
2. *Faith and Spirituality*: She leaned on her faith to find meaning and hope amidst adversity, often sharing her reflections on trusting a higher power.
3. *Focusing on Gratitude*: Despite her suffering, she emphasized finding beauty in small moments and practicing gratitude daily.
4. *Living Authentically*: Nightbirde inspired others by openly sharing her journey, demonstrating that vulnerability can be a source of strength and connection.

Nightbird's courage is a testament to the power of self-acceptance. Her words and music motivate people to find hope and purpose, even in the darkest times.

Escaping the Cycle of Self-Criticism

I've come to realize that emotional pain often traps us in an endless loop—a cycle of self-criticism and regret. As I mentioned in Chapter 3, we repeatedly replay our mistakes, desperately trying to rewrite the past. But this effort is as futile as a dog chasing its tail. No matter how much we struggle, we cannot change what happened. The past is immutable, and agonizing over it only keeps us stuck.

When you wrestle with a past event, part of you might believe that you were entirely in control and are alone to blame. But was it all your doing? Yes, something happened. But can we say with certainty that *you* made it happen, consciously and autonomously? The truth is life unfolds on its own accord.

Science supports this idea. In *Determined: A Science of Life Without Free Will*, Robert Sapolsky argues that human behavior isn't the result of autonomous choice but a complex interplay of biology, environment, and prior causes. He explains that our actions are shaped by genetics, brain activity, upbringing, and external circumstances. The choices we think we're making freely are, in reality, the outcome of interconnected forces beyond our conscious control. This challenges the notion of free will, reframing our actions as inevitable outcomes of life's intricate web.

Every experience, no matter how painful, serves a purpose in our journey. Instead of defending yourself against the accusations of your inner critic, you can break free of the loop by refusing to accept false narratives about yourself. There is no need to argue your innocence or justify your actions. Your reality is what it is: a blend of successes and failures, joy and sorrow, growth and setbacks. And borrowing from the Nightbird tradition is *okay*.

In the film *Enough* (2002), Jennifer Lopez's character, Slim Hiller, embodies this idea of self-compassion and determination. Facing her abusive, narcissistic husband, who threatened her life and harmed their daughter, Slim wrestled with whether she had the right to fight back. Her friend reminds her: *You have a divine animal right to protect your own life and the life of your offspring.* That right, as her friend continues, goes beyond mere physical survival. It includes the right to protect your emotional well-being and to pursue happiness.

I, too, remember the days when I had to declare that I was fighting for my life—not just to survive physically but to reclaim my happiness. Like Slim, I wasn't denying my imperfections but learning to embrace them. If you've endured emotional pain, you've likely had to fight for your survival, and you have every right to do so.

As Angelo Caerlang beautifully wrote, *Your imperfections remind you that you're still a human being who's continually becoming.* This journey isn't about perfection. It's about progress. It's about fighting for your happiness while accepting the full spectrum of who you are.

The Verdict of the Court

Should this court find me guilty of poor judgment, I will accept the verdict gracefully. However, I am reminded that guilt is not in harmony with the river of life. No sacred text anywhere in the world celebrates the value of guilt. Forgiveness—both from others and oneself—encompasses the energy of all that is divine and serves as the key to personal growth and progress. Therefore, I will tell my inner prosecutor: Thank you for pointing out my flaws, but your case contradicts Divine Law. My mistakes do not define me. My ability to learn, grow, and keep going defines me.

To anyone else standing trial in the court of their mind, I say this: Remember, you are not alone. We are all imperfect, and it is okay. You have the right to forgive yourself, to learn from your experiences, and to live a life filled with hope and possibility. It is written: You deserve love and kindness, forgiveness and compassion, and as many chances as necessary to discover your truth.

Worksheet

Step 1: Reflect on the Battle

Take a moment to reflect on this chapter. What did you learn about your mind's accusations?

Reflection Prompt: How does it feel to defend yourself and stand your ground? ____________

____

____

____

____

Step 2: Challenge your inner prosecutor by writing a compassionate letter of self-defense.

Emphasize your growth, intentions, and humanity. Example: "Yes, I made mistakes, but they don't define me. I've learned from them and taken steps to improve."

How would your inner defense lawyer respond? ___________________________

____

____

____

____

Step 3: The Scars of Sensitivity

Reflect on how your sensitivity has impacted your life positively and negatively.

A. The Positives of my Sensitivity (list)

____________________   ____________________

____________________   ____________________

____________________   ____________________

____________________   ____________________

B. The Negativities of Sensitivity (list)

____________________   ____________________

____________________   ____________________

_______________________ _______________________

_______________________ _______________________

C. Ways Sensitivity has hurt me (list)

_______________________ _______________________

_______________________ _______________________

_______________________ _______________________

_______________________ _______________________

Step 4: Make a Case for Forgiveness

D. Why do you think you need forgiveness?
   Free write your response. _______________

____

____

____

____

E. How will you know you've been forgiven?
   Free write your response. _______________

____

____

____

____

F. What step can you take today to move toward forgiveness? ______________________

____

____

____

____

Step 5: Breaking the Loop. Identify one recurring negative thought you need to release. Negative Loop Example: "I'll never be good enough." ______________________

____

____

____

____

Write a statement of liberation.

Liberating Statements: "I did not intend to cause harm to my children." ______________

____

____

____

____

Step 6: Releasing Guilt, Regret, and Shame (GRS). Dealing with GRS Syndrome:

A. Guilt

Reflection: Why do you feel guilty? (list as many as you want). _______________________

____

____

____

____

Decide if you have a valid reason to feel guilty.

Check One: Valid Guilt ____ False Guilt ____

Making Amends (What can you do to improve it, if possible?)

Acknowledge what you've done: __________
Can you reverse what you've done? Check One: Yes _____ No _____

Make amends, if possible. What can I do to make this right? _______________________

____

____

____

____

B. Regret

Why do you feel remorse? _______________
Acknowledge it: _________________________

Write a letter admitting what you've done and
share it if you feel it's important. _____________

____

____

____

____

C. Shame

Why do you feel shame? _______________
Acknowledge it _________________________

Write a letter admitting what you have done
and share it if you feel it is important. _________

____

____

____

____

Step 7: The Verdict: You are now the Jury

Guilty: _______________________

Innocent: _______________________

Step 8: Write one of these letters below.

A. Your Self-Acquittal Letter:
Now, it is time to forgive yourself.
Acknowledge the harm you've done, embrace
your humanity's imperfections, and permit
yourself to grow. Write a statement of self-acquittal that sets you free from guilt, regret, and
shame.
  Example:

"I, [Your Name], recognize that I am human.
Like others, I have made mistakes. I choose to
release the guilt, regret, and shame I've carried
and open myself to growth, understanding, and
self-compassion. My past does not define
me—I am defined by how I rise from it."

____

____

B. Self-Conviction Letter: _______________

In conclusion, self-compassion and for-giveness are crucial steps toward healing and growth. Recognizing that we are human means accepting that mistakes are inevitable on the journey of life. Condemning ourselves only deepens the wounds and reinforces the limiting beliefs that hold us back. Instead, by offering ourselves the same grace we would extend to a loved one, we can create space for growth and renewal.

Self-forgiveness is not about excusing mistakes but acknowledging our inherent worth and moving forward with kindness and understanding. Letting go of self-condemnation frees us to embrace new possibilities and rewrite our story with hope and intention, giving us a sense of purpose and optimism.

Chapter 6

Releasing Others' Opinions

Either they like you, or they don't. Never try to convince somebody of your worth. If a person doesn't appreciate you, they don't deserve you. Respect yourself and be with people who truly value you. Attributed to Denzel Washington

In the early 1990s, I stumbled upon Terry Cole-Whittaker's well-received book, *What You Think of Me Is None of My Business*. The book title immediately resonated with me. At that time, I was consumed by the idea that people didn't like me, and I believed their approval was crucial for my happiness and success.

This belief held me back from fully embracing my potential, particularly in my aspiration to become a public speaker. Cole-Whittaker's book introduced me to a liberating concept: our worth is not determined by other people's opinions. The author challenges us to break free from the need for validation and instead focus on self-empowerment, self-acceptance, and listening to our inner voice. She emphasizes that seeking external approval is a futile pursuit. True freedom, Cole-Whittaker teaches, is found in releasing the fear of judgment and living authentically, unshackled from the expectations of others.

Reflecting on those years, I now recognize how deeply ingrained my need for approval was. It was as if I walked around with an invisible sign that screamed, *I need your approval to be okay.* Over time, I've faced a hard but liberating truth: this neediness is a losing game. It often drives away the very people whose acceptance you crave. But relief comes with profound self-acceptance, offering a beacon of hope for those in emotional distress.

I vividly recall a conversation from the early 1980s when someone close to me bluntly said, "You turn people off." At first, her words stunned me, but I understood their painful accuracy over time. You can't force others to like you; you only lose yourself when you try.

Fawning

One of the most critical steps in breaking free from emotional distress is learning to surrender the need for constant approval. This is especially important if you find yourself "needy" in relationships—always seeking validation, attention, or affirmation from those around you.

Such behavior often takes the form of what psychologists refer to as *fawning*. This pattern involves excessive flattery, agreement, or self-sacrifice to gain acceptance and win favor. But breaking free from this pattern is empowering, leading to a sense of self-worth and independence.

While it might seem like you're simply being kind or supportive, the truth is that fawning often comes from a place of inauthenticity. It projects an energy of desperation rather than genuine care, ultimately hindering real connection and self-respect. Genuine care, on the other hand, is the cornerstone of healthy relationships, making both parties feel valued and respected.

Instead, it usually comes across as insincere when you present yourself as someone who wants something. People can sense when you're trying too hard to make them like you or befriend them. Your words might sound rehearsed, your actions might feel overly calculated, and your gestures may appear exaggerated. Whether you realize it or not, your underlying message is that you're not confident enough to be yourself, so you mold yourself to fit what you think others want.

However, this rarely works as intended. Ironically, fawning can often backfire, creating discomfort and even distrust. When your inauthenticity is detected, you risk being perceived as a fraud or manipulator, even if your intentions are purely for emotional security. This can lead to a sense of distance rather than connection, leaving you feeling more isolated or rejected, despite your efforts to please others.

The key to breaking free from emotional distress lies in releasing the desperate need for external approval. True confidence is cultivated from within, and as you learn to trust and validate yourself, you become less dependent on others for affirmation. When you stop striving to please everyone, you'll naturally attract relationships built on mutual respect and authenticity rather than fleeting or superficial validation. This shift, rooted in mutual respect, brings a sense of inner security and alignment with your true self, empowering you to live with greater freedom and authenticity. This sense of empowerment is the direct result of deep self-acceptance.

The Dale Carnegie Way

Networking for professional growth is crucial for establishing genuine connections across diverse disciplines and achieving success in any organization or endeavor. It can foster meaningful relationships that create shared knowledge for mutually beneficial collaborations, fostering mutual growth and expansion opportunities.

To establish authentic connections with others, being genuine and showing interest in them is important rather than just focusing on what you can gain. For example, you can ask open-ended questions, listen actively, and offer help or support when needed. Such connections are the foundation for long-term growth and achievement in business, politics, or any other field. Writers, speakers, and leaders champion this principle, emphasizing that authentic networking is not about flattery or seeking personal gain but creating lasting, valuable alliances.

In his groundbreaking book *How to Win Friends and Influence People*, Dale Carnegie, a pioneering figure in the early twentieth-century self-help movement, presents a timeless approach to cultivating meaningful relationships. In the early 1980s, when life was difficult, I enrolled in the Dale Carnegie Course, taking stock of my insecurities and expressing a strong desire to grow. This transformative program is designed to unlock an individual's potential by honing essential communication, leadership, and interpersonal skills—qualities I felt I was lacking at the time.

The course emphasized the development of self-confidence and emotional intelligence. These concepts are widely accepted today, but were truly revolutionary at the time. It underscored the belief that anyone could develop practical relationship-building skills, empowering them to navigate personal and professional challenges more easily. Through practical techniques for managing stress, enhancing public speaking skills, and cultivating genuine connections, the course provides indispensable tools for achieving success in any field.

It is essential to recognize a critical distinction between the concept of fawning and Carnegie's approach. Fawning stems from insecurity and manifests as an unconscious attempt to gain affection or validation, often at the cost of one's self-worth. It's driven by a fear of rejection or an overwhelming need for approval.

In contrast, Carnegie's principles are grounded in empathy and mutual respect. He advocates active listening, recognizing others' strengths, and offering sincere praise. His approach fosters trust and connection without compromising one's authenticity or independence. While fawning seeks validation through manipulation or self-sacrifice, Carnegie's method cultivates healthier, more balanced interactions. It's about treating others with kindness and respect because we genuinely acknowledge their inherent worth.

This recognition is central to Carnegie's philosophy. Seeing and appreciating others for who they are makes them feel valued and re-spected. Furthermore, this isn't manipulation; it's a sincere expression of interest in the well-being of others. By focusing on the needs and strengths of others without ulterior motives, we can cultivate relationships built on mutual respect, where the emphasis shifts from seeking validation to offering genuine sincerity.

According to Carnegie, authentic connections don't arise from flattering others or seeking approval. They come from being fully present with them, engaged, and without pretense. In doing so, we build relationships in which everyone feels respected for who they are—not for what they can offer in return.

Venting vs. Complaining

Dr. Rachel Millstein, a clinical health psychologist at Harvard Medical School, promotes venting as a strategy for managing stress. She notes that sharing feelings with an empathetic listener can strengthen social connections. As Millstein states, "Calling a friend and letting it out can be helpful." Venting can help us feel connected to our support networks, significantly impacting our life satisfaction and overall well-being.

However, while venting can promote our emotional well-being, Millstein advises doing so thoughtfully to avoid reinforcing negative emotions. She said that to ensure venting remains productive, it's essential to approach it with purpose. Venting without seeking a resolution can sometimes reinforce negativity rather than alleviate it.

When you're in emotional distress and feeling pain, it can seem like the world is conspiring against you. You might struggle to be authentic, caught in an endless cycle where, when things don't go as expected, you shift into blaming others for how you perceive they've treated you. While this might feel like a natural outlet for your pain, it rarely provides lasting relief. Ultimately, no one can make you feel good about yourself; that power belongs to you.

This chapter encourages you to face your emotional wounds directly— not by denying or suppressing them, but by acknowledging them honestly and with compassion. Recognizing your pain is not a sign of weakness but an essential step toward healing. It's important to understand that your pain is valid, and acknowledging it is a powerful affirmation of your worth. By expressing the hurt you feel—whether from the actions of others or circumstances—within a safe, confidential, and supportive environment, you open yourself up to new possibilities for healing, growth, and empowerment. In doing so, you reclaim control over your mental and emotional well-being.

As we explored in Chapter 5, justice is often associated with legal systems with judges, courts, juries, and lawyers. However, emotional justice is a deeply personal journey. It resides within your thoughts, feelings, and experiences and is intricately connected to the narrative of your life. You may find yourself replaying moments when others have hurt you, especially when you feel unsupported or dismissed by them.

This chapter offers you the tools to reframe this narrative. Investigate and process your emotional wounds. Rather than blaming others or seeking revenge, this process invites you to take a step back and assess your feelings of hurt so you can acknowledge your pain and, ultimately, reclaim your power.

Emotional healing isn't about seeking punishment or justice in the conventional sense. It's about understanding, validating, and honoring your experience. Your path toward healing is deeply personal, empowering you to cultivate a greater sense of control and peace. This chapter is your refuge, a space to express yourself fully and honestly without judgment. Within these pages, you can release the weight you've been carrying—all the frustrations, disappointments, anger, and judgment.

However, it's vital to distinguish between venting and complaining. While there may be a therapeutic value of venting, complaining focuses on external factors and can trap you in unproductive "vicious cycles," as Dr. Low observed. In contrast, venting allows you to acknowledge and release your internal emotions.

My training with the Recovery Method highlighted the importance of this distinction. Dr. Low, for example, would raise his hands when patients came to his office to complain, signaling them to stop. He recognized that chronic complaining often deepened emotional distress, so he introduced the "five-minute rule."

This simple yet powerful technique empowers individuals to express their feelings freely, providing a structured approach to emotional release. Still, it encourages them to move beyond the habit of complaining. This distinction is pivotal for emotional release and healing. Venting is not about dwelling on negativity but processing your emotions to gain clarity, ultimately allowing you to move forward in a positive way.

Thus, venting can be a healthy way to acknowledge and deal with your feelings rather than letting them fester or become resentful. Venting isn't just a cathartic release; it's a valuable emotional tool for promoting mental health. Psychologists and psychiatrists often recommend it because it allows us to process and externalize complicated feelings.

Dr. James Pennebaker, a leading researcher on emotional expression, has found that writing or talking about emotions can significantly reduce stress and improve overall mental well-being. Venting helps to "unclog" emotional blockages, releasing tension and providing clarity.

In my work with therapists, they frequently use venting to help clients gain perspective and insight into their emotions and develop healthier coping strategies. Dr. John M. Grohol, a psychologist and founder of Psych Central, notes that expressing feelings openly can help people in emotional distress feel more in control of their emotions, preventing them from becoming bottled up and turning into anxiety or depression. This empowerment is a key benefit of venting.

So, rather than discouraging the practice of venting, we wholeheartedly invite you to embrace it. First, reflect on all the people you believe are responsible for some of the emotional pain you've experienced. It's not about right or wrong or whether they would agree with you. Create your list by writing down the names of the people who hurt you in a private place. This is your opportunity to be brutally honest. Don't censor yourself or downplay the significance of any encounter. Whether it's a casual acquaintance, a close friend, or a family member, they belong on this list if their actions or words hurt you.

Take your time with this step. Go back through your memories and record them all, asking yourself:

- Who made you feel invisible or unworthy?
- Who dismissed your feelings or undermined your confidence?
- Who betrayed your trust or failed you when you needed them most?
- Who criticized you harshly or unfairly?
- Who excluded you, gossiped about you, or judged you?
- Who abandoned you?
- Who condemned you with hurtful epithets?

If this exercise triggers any negative emotions in you, let it all out by sobbing, shouting, or doing whatever else you need to do. Remember, putting it on paper is a safe space to express your feelings. Once again, write down every name that comes to mind, no matter how insignificant the offense may seem at the moment. Emotional wounds can stem from minor events, so don't dismiss how you feel. The goal of this exercise is not to dwell on past hurts but to recognize their origins. You are safe here on paper, and your healing is our priority.

Examine the Impact

Do you remember the phrase, "Sticks and stones may break my bones, but words will never hurt me"? I looked it up and discovered that this rhyme has existed since the nineteenth century. Well-meaning adults likely used it to encourage children to resist the emotional impact of bullying, including name-calling and taunts. It emphasizes the importance of strength of character in dismissing verbal insults while suggesting that physical harm, such as broken bones, is more damaging than words.

However, trained mental health professionals are better equipped to know this. Carl Jung, the pioneering Swiss psychiatrist, thought otherwise. He believed that words and language are powerful because they can tap into unconscious thoughts and feelings, even when we are unaware of them. Words can have a profound impact on the psyche, shaping one's sense of self, beliefs, and emotional health. For Jung, words can hurt us and strike a deeper wound if we are already in emotional distress. In that state, we may believe the words thrown at us, even if they are untrue.

William James, another pioneering figure in psychology, also believed that words can leave a lasting negative impact on one's sense of self-worth. He taught that, as rational beings, our emotions and personal experiences shape our perception of the world. James believed that self-esteem often comes from external sources, including the negative judgments of others. Therefore, Jung and James would agree that words can hurt, especially if one lacks a healthy sense of self-worth.

Furthermore, you are in good company if you believe that something said to you hurt you. Psychologists and many modern-day mental health professionals would agree with you. For example, the Adverse Childhood Experiences Study (ACE) concluded that the trauma of children is predictive of whether they graduate from high school, struggle with addiction, or end up incarcerated. While the ACE study underscores the role of childhood trauma in shaping our early development, it also acknowledges that human factors like healthy self-esteem can help individuals overcome adversity.

Therefore, we must recognize that emotional wounds can persist and continue to impact us if left untreated. Hence, there is nothing wrong with you if you believe someone caused you emotional harm. However, we cannot afford to let the hurt caused by others hold us back or use it as an excuse for our behavior. We want to understand the situation and overcome emotional distress.

Moving Forward

As you continue your journey of personal growth, remember this essential truth: while validation from others can be comforting, it is ultimately an unreliable source of lasting peace and confidence. If others can validate you, they also have the power to withdraw it. As Dr. Low teaches, practice self-endorsement. External validation is fleeting, subjective, and ultimately unsatisfying. The most transformative shift you can make is turning inward—nurturing self-respect and embracing your authentic self.

I've discussed releasing and letting go throughout this book and several times in this chapter. Therapists and coaches often emphasize the importance of letting go of the past to make space for something new. But what does it mean to release and let go? And how do we do it?

Early one Sunday morning, as I lay in bed, immobilized by depression, a voice on the radio cut through the haze. The message was meant for me because they don't usually advertise over the radio. The voice was Lester Levinson's—at least, a recording of him—the creator of the Sedona Method. He spoke with clarity about the power of releasing. I didn't fully understand what he meant, but something in me stirred. It was as if a door cracked open inside me, and I felt, maybe for the first time, that it might be possible to let go of my emotional pain.

Curious, I typed a few keywords into an Internet search. That led me to Sedona Associates. I later found that they offered cassette-based courses for learning and practicing the

Sedona Method. I got one and began listening, then participated in self-help seminars.

The Sedona Method is a powerful self-inquiry technique for emotional release and inner freedom, rooted in the art of letting go. Lester developed it to help us recognize and release unwanted emotions, thoughts, and limiting beliefs. The Sedona Method uses simple yet profound questions to guide individuals in willingly releasing emotional baggage, rather than suppressing or resisting it.

Central to the Sedona Method is the understanding that emotions are not permanent, and we can release them once we see they are not who we truly are. Through consistent practice, individuals can experience greater peace, clarity, and empowerment. Over time, the Sedona Method can dissolve internal blocks and support lasting transformation, enabling people to respond to life more freely and with less reactivity.

If you need assistance practicing releasing, the Sedona Method could help. When you release the grip of the opinions of others, you experience true freedom. In this state, your self-worth no longer depends on external approval. This freedom creates space for deeper, more meaningful connections and relationships built on mutual respect and shared authenticity.

Ultimately, you will uplift your "tribe," and they will do the same for you without needing validation from those not genuinely aligned with your values. Be true to yourself; the right people will naturally be drawn to you. Their respect and appreciation will stem from a genuine connection, not from a need for external validation. This shift brings profound relief and liberation. By freeing yourself from the pursuit of approval, you'll witness a remarkable transformation in your life.

Therapeutic Letters

Writing therapeutic letters is a powerful tool for emotional healing and self-expression. When you've been hurt by someone, writing a letter can provide a meaningful outlet for your feelings. The goal is not to seek validation or a response from the person who caused you pain but to express your emotions honestly and release the hurt.

This process allows you to externalize your pain, gain clarity on your emotions, and heal. It's a way of taking back your power—not by trying to change the other person, but by reclaiming your emotional well-being. Writing letters offers a cathartic release, helping you achieve emotional freedom and healing.

A therapeutic letter to yourself is the most important one you'll ever write. No matter how committed you are to healing, there will be moments when you forget how far you've come. You'll slip back into self-blame, wish for a different life, and feel the weight of shame, guilt, and worry. When that happens, take a moment to write to yourself. Review your thought process at the time and explain why you acted the way you did. Remind yourself of your strengths and positive qualities. One letter might not be enough—write as many as you need. Then, when the emotional storms hit, read those letters. Allow them to lift your spirits, improve your mood, and help you reconnect with the goodness in your life.

When writing therapeutic letters to others, list the individuals who have harmed you. Then, write a letter to each one. Don't worry about whether they'll ever read the letter; it's only for your eyes only. What matters is that you acknowledge your feelings and give them a place to exist. Let it flow freely onto the page, whether it's anger, sadness, confusion, betrayal, or any other emotion. Use this exercise to confront those who wronged you, even if it's only in your mind. Here are a few prompts to get you started:

- *When you said/did _____________________, it made me feel _____________________.*
- *I've carried the pain of your actions for years, making me feel _____________________.*

These letters allow you to organize your emotions, acknowledge, and release your pain. Write as many letters as you need, and don't hold back. Let the words flow without concern for anyone else's feelings; this is your healing space.

1. *Confront Trusted Figures*

Some names on your list may be challenging, especially if they held positions of trust or authority, such as teachers, mentors, clergy, or even family members. It's painful to recognize that these individuals, who should have supported and nurtured you, may have contributed to your hurt. You might hesitate to write about them, thinking it's somehow a betrayal or an unfair judgment of their entire character. But this exercise isn't about blaming them for everything. It's about giving yourself the space to acknowledge how their actions impacted you. For instance:

- *A teacher's dismissive comment might have shattered your self-confidence.*
- *A religious leader's negative opinion could have made you feel unworthy.*
- *A family member's neglect might have left you feeling unloved or unsupported.*

Addressing these hurts doesn't negate any positive aspects of these relationships; it simply validates your emotional experience. Allow yourself to process these feelings and recognize that your hurt is real, regardless of the person's intentions.

2. Friends and Acquaintances

It's not only family and authority figures who can hurt us—friends and acquaintances can also cause emotional distress. Friendships are built on trust and care, but even the closest friends may disappoint us. Maybe they gossiped about you, excluded you from something important, or failed to support you during a difficult time. When writing letters to friends, ask yourself:

- *Have I been holding onto resentment because of their actions?*
- *Am I avoiding addressing this hurt because I value friendship?*
- *How can I honor my feelings while still preserving the relationship?*

Writing letters to friends is not about ending the relationship; it's about creating clarity and releasing unresolved tension. This process can help you decide whether the relationship still serves you or needs to evolve.

3. *Family and Upbringing*

Family dynamics are often the most complex and emotionally charged. Our families shape our earliest experiences and influence how we perceive ourselves and the world. Writing about family members can bring up deep, sometimes painful emotions, especially if you've experienced neglect, abuse, or a lack of emotional support.

When writing to family members, focus on specific actions and how they impacted you. For example:

- *When you constantly compare me to my siblings, it makes me feel inadequate.*
- *When you dismissed my dreams and ambitions, I doubted my abilities.*

This step is not about blaming your family for all your struggles; it's about understanding how their behavior affected your emotional development. By identifying these wounds, you reclaim control over your healing process.

4. *Writing to Your Parents*

Writing to parents, especially your mother, may feel like a betrayal. Mothers occupy a special place in our hearts: they are often the first source of love and care, but they are also human and imperfect. Reflecting on your relationship with your mother may evoke a complex blend of gratitude and resentment. It's possible to love your mother deeply and still acknowledge that she may have caused you pain, intentionally or not.

Likewise, your relationship with your father may bring different emotions, but it, too, deserves attention. Whether you're writing to express hurt, frustration, or even gratitude, allow yourself to be honest. Reflect on how their actions—or inactions—impacted you.

Once you've written your letters, pause, breathe, and reflect on what surfaced. Writing these letters is just the beginning of your healing journey. The next crucial step is releasing the emotional energy associated with these experiences. Let go of the mental weight of past hurts. This practice empowers you to reclaim your narrative and take back control over your emotional well-being. The goal is peace, and this chapter serves as your roadmap to get there. With each step, you'll feel lighter and more liberated as you release this emotional energy.

Remember, writing letters isn't about holding onto resentment or anger. It's about freeing yourself from their grip. Once you've been confronted with the sources of your pain, the next step is to release emotional energy tied to those memories. Let go of the mental weight of past hurts. This practice empowers you to reclaim your narrative and take back control over your emotional well-being. The goal is personal peace, and this chapter serves as your roadmap to get there. Stay hopeful and motivated, knowing that peace is within reach.

The Dynamics of Relationships

Here's a simple truth: Not everyone will like you, and that's perfectly okay. Some people won't "click" with you. That's a natural part of life. It's not about hatred or ill will; it's just how relationships work. Think about it: do you genuinely like everyone you meet? Probably not. And that's fine too. It doesn't mean you wish them harm or hold ill feelings; it just means there's no connection with them. You're not alone in this—everyone experiences this feeling of being drawn to some and repelled by others.

For example, I once bought a golf cart from a store where the owner and I didn't connect. Something about our interaction was off, and I felt the same on a later visit. It wasn't that I disliked him, and I'm sure he didn't dislike me—it was simply a matter of incompatibility. I wouldn't choose him as a friend, but that doesn't mean I wish him harm.

Here's the takeaway: It's okay not to like everyone and equally okay if others don't want you. Once you accept this, you'll stop wasting energy on relationships that aren't meant to be and focus on those that truly matter. This shift in focus empowers you to engage with people who genuinely align with your values, creating a sense of control over your social interactions.

People Don't Think About You as Much as You Think

Byron Katie often highlights the three types of business we face: God's business, other people's business, and your business. When you worry about what others think, you're invading their business. How often do you obsess over someone else's life, choices, or opinions? For most of us, the answer is rarely, if ever. Instead, our minds are consumed with our concerns and responsibilities. This realization can be liberating.

When you stop worrying about what others think, you free up energy and mental space for what truly matters—your life. It's not personal; it's just life. This shift in mindset helps you feel less self-conscious and more at ease in social situations.

At a fundamental level, most people are not looking to harm you. Most harmful actions stem from thoughtlessness, misunderstandings, or a lack of awareness, rather than malice. If you were to ask a stranger for help, whether for directions or a meal, you'd likely experience kindness.

This simple truth underscores the idea that most people aren't out to hurt you. Recognize that many hurtful actions may seem benign, and this awareness alone will empower you to reframe your perspective on negative interactions. Instead of assuming ill intent, consider the possibility that the other person didn't know better or wasn't thinking clearly. This revision lets you express yourself more naturally, without worrying about how others perceive you.

It's easy to assume that others intentionally hurt us. However, many people are unaware of the impact their actions have on others. Their behavior might be careless or inconsiderate, but it's rarely malicious. As someone with a physical disability, I've experienced moments of frustration when others seemed inconsiderate.

For example, I became angry at a conference when the organizers failed to provide adequate accommodation for attendees with disabilities. Healthy individuals stood idly by as others with walkers and canes struggled to navigate the event. I had a similar experience at a mega church. I felt the greeters up front looked away as I waddled with my walker. At first, I was furious. However, upon reflection, I realized they didn't fully understand our challenges. Their oversight wasn't malicious; it resulted from a lack of awareness.

Understanding this doesn't excuse poor behavior, but helps you release resentment. When you see others as human, flawed, and imperfect, you free yourself from the emotional weight of their actions.

Four Core Lessons

I initially learned about the brain's neuroplasticity from the book *Evolve Your Brain: The Science of Changing Your Mind* by Dr. Joe Dispenza. Dr. Joe is a chiropractor and neuroscientist focusing on the relationship between thoughts, emotions, and the brain's ability to change.

He and many other neuroscientists suggest that reprogramming the brain is rooted in its ability to adapt and form new neural connections over time. Changing deeply ingrained thought patterns, habits, or emotional responses requires consistent effort and practice. Introducing these simple exercises will cement what we have learned and serve as stepping stones to further emotional healing:

1. *Not everyone will like you, and you won't like everyone.* Accepting this truth is liberating. Dr. Albert Ellis, the creator of Rational Emotive Behavior Therapy (REBT), taught his clients how to manage or reframe irrational beliefs. Ellis often emphasized that striving for universal approval is both unrealistic and counterproductive. In REBT, he taught that accepting that not everyone will like you is essential for emotional well-being.

   Dr. Ellis might also say their behavior is not personal to you and encourage you to reframe your automatic response.

2. *Past experiences and conditioning shape your present behavior, reactions, and thoughts.* Michael Singer, the author of *The Untethered Soul,* reminds us that psychology suggests that our past conditioning often governs our lives. Thus, our mind and body respond to the world around us based on the accumulation of these past experiences, frequently trapping us in automatic patterns.

This can lead us to react unconsciously rather than thoughtfully choosing how to respond. Trying to control external events and people typically stems from an inner belief that we can orchestrate every aspect of our lives. It's easy to blame others for our circumstances, but Singer reminds us that we look in the wrong direction when we focus outwardly. We often think our problems are caused by someone else, but that's not true.

Breaking free from this conditioning is possible through your power of awareness. Recognizing and becoming aware of your thoughts and emotions can help you transcend automatic reactions, allowing you to experience life with greater freedom and presence. This awareness is the key to unlocking a more hopeful future.

Singer offers a liberating idea: "You are not your thoughts; you are the one who is aware of your thoughts. You are not your emotions; you are the one who is aware of your emotions. You are not your past experiences; you are the one who is aware of your experiences." This maxim can liberate us from the shackles of our past, enabling us to seize opportunities for personal growth.

3. *Most people don't intend to hurt others in everyday life.* Assume good intentions unless proven otherwise. Dr. Abraham Low is well-known for his self-help and mental health recovery work. One of his core teachings is encapsulated in the idea that "people don't aim at you," which emphasizes the need to reinterpret interpersonal conflicts and misunderstandings to reduce emotional distress.

   Dr. Low's statement highlights the notion that the actions or words of others are often not intended as personal attacks, even if they may be perceived as such. It reminds us to avoid taking things personally and to understand that people's behaviors are frequently driven by their internal struggles, misunderstandings, or momentary states of mind rather than a deliberate intent to harm or target someone. *People often act out of ignorance, not malice.* So, don't take offense too quickly.

   Dr. Low would ask if you wanted peace or power. If you want peace, you'll realize that the individual was not aiming at you; they did not intend to cause you harm but acted out of their emotions, which they don't understand.

4. *What others do may stimulate our feelings, but not the cause.* Dr. Marshall Rosenberg, known for Nonviolent Communication (NVC), taught that people's actions often stem from their unmet needs and limited awareness rather than their intent to harm us. He encouraged compassionate communication to uncover and address those underlying needs. When someone lashes out, Rosenberg might suggest interpreting it as a reflection of their pain or ignorance rather than an attack.

By internalizing these core lessons, you allow people to be human. You release the expectation that others must behave in a certain way to make you feel good. This freedom is a gift you give yourself.

These ideas also underscore emotional intelligence, as suggested by Attorney Patrice Borders, the founder of Amplify Emotional Intelligence. When we interpret other people's actions through a lens of ignorance rather than malice, we are less likely

to react with hostility and more likely to respond with empathy and patience. This simple but profound shift improves interpersonal relationships, emotional intelligence,
and mental well-being.

Chapter 7

Moral Injury

Moral injury is the wound that occurs when one betrays one's own moral beliefs, either by doing something that violates them, or by failing to prevent something that violates them. Jonathan Shay

When we hurt others, especially in ways that conflict with our core values, the emotional toll can be far more significant than we expect. This is where the concept of *moral injury* comes in. Moral injury refers to the psychological distress that arises when our intentional or accidental actions violate our sense of what is right.

Unlike typical feelings of guilt or remorse, moral injury is deeply rooted in a profound moral and ethical conflict. It's the internal battle between who we believe to be and what we've done. The emotional hurt we feel from moral injury is not just about causing harm to another person; it's about damage to our sense of integrity and identity. In a nutshell, it's about the emotional pain we cause ourselves because of the harm or wrong we believe we've done to someone else.

Maryann Jacobi Gray was a social psychologist who delivered a moving TEDx Talk several years ago. I first discovered her work during a time of deep emotional pain when I turned to YouTube in search of something to help me cope. Her words resonated deeply with me, especially when she described the struggle of dealing with the pain of having hurt someone else. We also shared a personal connection: we studied at the same university in Oxford, Ohio. There, a life-altering event—entirely out of her control—took place in that small college town. I'll share more about that later.

After the incident, which included a lengthy investigation, Maryann moved to California, where she completed her education. With her expertise in social psychology, she became a writer, professor, and university administrator. Her story stayed with me for a long time, and as a podcaster, I wanted to have her on my show to talk about her work. Unfortunately,

Maryann passed away before that could happen.

Still, her insights into moral injury continue to influence my understanding of the pain many of us carry when we believe we have caused harm to others. But before we dive into the event that changed Maryann's life, let's first examine what moral injury is and how it shapes our perceptions of ourselves and others when we believe we've caused the suffering of others.

The Meaning of Moral Injury

Moral injury can arise in various situations, each involving a clash between one's actions—or, in some cases, inactions—and deeply held moral principles. It occurs when individuals perceive that they have transgressed their ethical code or when they are involved in events that contradict their values. The impact of this injury can be profound, and the experience often leaves an enduring emotional scar. Let's explore several scenarios illustrating how moral injury can manifest in a person's life, ranging from seemingly minor incidents to life-altering events.

Take, for example, the case of Maryann. She was involved in a life-altering event, but it wasn't because of anything she did wrong. An investigation later confirmed that she wasn't negligent and that her actions didn't directly cause the tragic outcome. Still, just being part of the accident left her carrying a heavy emotional burden. Even though she wasn't at fault, she couldn't shake the feeling that she'd failed somehow. It's a feeling many people with moral injury know all too well, especially when their values clash with the complex realities of a situation.

Or think about a sober driver who, in a split second of distraction, misses a traffic light and causes a serious accident. They weren't drunk or high; they were entirely in control of the car. But in that fleeting moment, someone else's life is changed forever. The weight of that moment can be crushing—not just because of what happened, but because the driver feels like their brief lapse, no matter how small, led to someone else's suffering. The pain they carry is often not only from the consequences but from the moral injury they experience: the feeling that their failure to uphold the highest standard of responsibility harmed another person.

Moral injury can also appear in situations that seem more mundane but are emotionally significant. Consider the case of someone going through a divorce. The person seeking divorce may later feel intense guilt or regret, particularly when they witness the pain it causes their spouse, children, or extended family. Even if the decision was right for them, the moral injury comes from the emotional fallout and the harm they feel they've caused others.

The person may question their actions and feel torn between doing what they thought was right and the hurt they've caused. Similarly, a student who cheats on a test and later feels guilty about it or a professional who makes a mistake at work and feels responsible for the consequences is experiencing a moral injury.

In a more extreme scenario, imagine a soldier in a combat situation who feels responsible for the deaths of non-combatants. Even if the soldier followed orders and acted within the rules of engagement, the moral injury in this case may stem from the belief that their actions directly contributed to the loss of innocent lives. The mental and emotional toll of these situations can be immense, leading to feelings of shame, guilt, and endless self-recrimination.

Do you see where I'm going with this? Moral injury can occur at many different levels, from serious, life-altering events like Maryann's to seemingly small but emotionally significant ones like a divorce. It may also stem from actions we directly take, the consequences of those actions, or situations where we feel complicit, even when we have no control over the outcome. The effects can be long-lasting, and the struggle to reconcile our sense of self with the harm we believe we've caused is a central part of the experience.

In the following sections, I'll explore the different layers and levels of moral injury, ranging from the most devastating to those that, although perhaps less severe, still leave a lasting impact on our psyche. The journey through moral injury is not linear, and healing takes time, understanding, and, often, support from others who can help us make sense of our emotional pain. Healing from moral injury involves acknowledging the harm caused, accepting responsibility, and finding ways to live by your values despite past actions.

Conscientious to a Fault

Upon completing my master's degree, one of my professors told me I was conscientious to a fault. He pegged me right because my profile included being prone to seeing assaults on my character as unfair, having the penchant to criticize myself, and the belief that there is a right and wrong. While I didn't know it at the time, my personality suggests that I may be someone who is prone to experiencing moral injury.

Mental health professionals have explored moral injury, indicating that it is often linked to certain personality traits, mental health conditions, and a lack of practical coping skills. These individuals also tend to have an exaggerated sense of morality and may feel compelled to always do or say the right thing.

When I was involved in training for life coaches, one participant shared that a client of his had died by suicide. At the time, I didn't know much about moral injury, but in retrospect, it was clear that the coach was questioning his skills, wondering if there was something more he could have done.

I also witnessed the pain we suffered when I lost my first son. His doctor had examined him just a few months prior and had pronounced him fit and strong, but he collapsed on the football field, never to recover. The doctor came to see him, and we could all see how deeply shaken he was by the loss. The hospital doctor told us that his colleague, who had been involved in my son's care, also felt the weight of the loss.

Psychiatrists suggest that individuals with a high sense of responsibility are particularly vulnerable to moral injury because they internalize the responsibility for someone's well-being. When something goes wrong, especially if it involves harming others, their sense of duty can turn inward, often leading to intense guilt and failure. In medicine today, for example, many doctors have opened up about burnout in the healthcare profession. This can contribute to heightened anxiety, depression, and even PTSD-like symptoms. Some doctors, among the best educated of all professionals, also die by suicide. This could involve many factors, but we can't discount moral injury.

However, not everyone experiences moral injury when they fail to meet societal expectations. Some fathers, for instance, may abandon their children without assuming responsibility for their care. Some men may have multiple children with different women, yet they do not feel responsible for any of them. Similarly, women may have children and then send them to their mothers to be raised.

Moreover, specialized soldiers, like snipers, may perform their duties in war and feel that their primary responsibility is to protect their comrades, even if their actions lead to the deaths of combatants. For example, the 2014 film *American Sniper* highlights the tension between performing a job that harms others and the emotional consequences that follow. The movie suggested that some people have personality traits and a mindset that allows them to avoid moral conflict and process their actions to prevent significant emotional distress.

In the movie, Chris Kyle, played by Bradley Cooper, told a hospital therapist, "It was my duty to shoot the enemy, and I don't regret it. What haunts me is all the guys I couldn't save." With such a mindset, Chris would not experience moral injury for his acts as a soldier. From how the movie portrayed him, he might have had emotional distress because he felt obligated to save more of his men on the battlefield. Therefore, the emotion of moral injury is highly complex, and it is difficult to predict who will experience it or why.

Maryann Jacobi Gray's Story

Maryann Jacobi Gray's TEDx Talk was my first introduction to moral injury, and it remains the most vivid discussion of the subject I've ever encountered. Maryann spoke openly about the emotional distress she experienced after an incident in Oxford while she was a graduate student. I've revisited her story many times, and it still chokes me because I can feel the weight of her moral injury.

Maryann accidentally hit and killed an eight-year-old boy named Brian. The boy innocently ran into the street, and she could not stop the car before it struck him. She describes how, although she was not legally at fault, she felt a profound sense of responsibility for his death. This tragedy haunted her for a long time. She spent many years keeping the incident a secret, unable to fully process the emotional pain and guilt until much later in her life.

Maryann starts the speech by drawing from the story of the Greek god Apollo. He had everything, she said, "Apollo was among the most beautiful and virtuous of all the gods. He was an amazing athlete. He had the gift of prophecy. He was a poet and a musician."

But Apollo had accidentally killed his lover, Hyacinth. While he tried to use all his powers to save his lover, it would not be. If Apollo couldn't prevent a tragic accident, she asked, how can we mere mortals do so? She then takes us into a deep reflection on how even the best intentions can lead to harm and how such moments of unintentional wrongdoing can profoundly disrupt lives and relationships.

Maryann then shifts to a broader discussion of moral injury, explaining that it can often lead to a social disconnect. Whether from a tragic accident like hers or less severe mistakes, such as those made by Amy Poehler, an American actress and comedian who performed the skit "The Clumsy Guy" on *Saturday Night Live* (SNL). Poehler and others involved in the show initially believed it would be humorous to mimic and exaggerate how people with disabilities navigate their surroundings.

However, the routine backfired, and many people considered it highly offensive. While she did not immediately "get it," Poehler later apologized for her part in the show, realizing it hurts to hurt others.

After earning the doctorate at a California institution, Maryann spent much of her professional career studying the effects of moral injury. She examined both ends of the spectrum, considering how it impacted the perpetrator and the community. She explains that while most minor mistakes can be corrected, some incidents may cause profound, irreversible harm. These emotional or physical wounds, whether inflicted by accident or not, leave both parties feeling hurt and often result in guilt, shame, and isolation for the person who caused the harm.

Healing Moral Injury

Maryann Jacobi Gray's experience with moral injury provides a poignant personal reflection on the pain of unintentionally harming others and offers a valuable framework for healing and moving forward. Gray identifies three key strategies for addressing moral injury, based on her research and personal experiences: accountability, compassion, and community service. When put into practice, these strategies can help restore a healthy sense of balance to our nervous system and foster connection after causing emotional or physical harm:

- *Accountability (Acknowledging the Harm)*: Taking responsibility is crucial in healing from moral injury. This involves openly acknowledging the harm caused, whether to the person directly affected or their loved ones. However, admitting the injury we've caused can be incredibly difficult. Still, as Maryanne points out, it is an essential part of the healing process.

Owning our mistakes allows us to confront our emotional distress and take a step toward a resolution.

This concept is not new; it has been explored in literature for centuries. Take Shakespeare's *Othello*, for example. Othello admits to his devastating act in the play, which resulted in the death of his lover: "Twas I that killed her." This decisive moment shows that recognizing the wrong we've done, no matter how painful, can lead to emotional clarity and, ultimately, relief. It's about facing the truth, no matter how uncomfortable, and allowing ourselves the space to feel remorse and guilt. While it may be challenging to face, this accountability is the foundation for emotional healing.

- *Compassion (Showing Empathy, Especially for Yourself)*: While accountability is about recognizing the harm done to others, compassion is about recognizing the pain within ourselves. When we experience moral injury, we often feel overwhelmed by guilt, shame, and self-condemnation.

It's easy to become trapped in a cycle of negative self-judgment.

Portia Louder, an author, speaker, formerly incarcerated person, and social media influencer on LinkedIn, shared a powerful encounter with an individual she met in federal prison. The incarcerated woman, despite a life of unimaginable hardships that began on the streets at just 11 years old, showed remarkable strength and resilience. Her mother had forced her into prostitution to feed her drug habit, and she had endured years in and out of foster care. She developed innumerable problems, which eventually landed her in prison.

While she had many reasons to blame her mother for the harm she had caused, she still expressed compassion for her. When her mother was dying of AIDS, she tried to apologize to her daughter. Portia's friend recalled, "The memories were so painful, she couldn't even get the words out." Even at the end of her life, her mother couldn't forgive herself. This was a classic case of moral injury. This emotional and psychological toll comes from actions that violate our deeply held moral beliefs.

But the story doesn't end in tragedy. Despite her imprisonment and all the emotional pain she endured, the daughter demonstrated a genuinely moving act of compassion and forgiveness. With tears in her eyes, Portia said she listened attentively as her friend recounted her story, then said, "Momma, it's time to let it go. I'm doing good; find you some peace."

Then, with profound grace, Portia said her friend turned to comfort her: "She reached over, hugged me, and said, 'It's okay, honey, don't be sad; God's been so good to me. I got my GED in prison and made some good friends." Maryanne, whom she had never met, might have identified with their suffering. I also believe she would recognize both the depth of pain caused by moral injury and the freedom that comes from compassion and forgiveness.

To truly heal from moral injury, we must learn to practice compassion for others and ourselves. Mental health professionals often emphasize the crucial role of self-compassion in emotional healing. Compassion is the recognition that, as humans, we are imperfect, and at times, we will fall short of our ideals and fail others. To heal, we must offer ourselves the same kindness, understanding, and forgiveness we would extend to a loved one in a similar situation. This self-compassion is not just helpful; it's essential for navigating the emotional turmoil of moral injury and can provide the foundation for personal growth and recovery.

- *Community Service (Reconnecting and Making Amends):* The third essential strategy involves *community service*, which means reconnecting with others and, when possible, making amends. When we cause harm, it's tempting to withdraw in guilt and shame, futilely attempting to hide from the world and from those we've hurt.

However, as Maryann Jacobi Gray points out, this isolation only deepens the sense of alienation that comes with moral injury. Instead of retreating, she advises that we find ways to re-engage with the community and offer something positive in return. Service is medicinal because it forces us to look out instead of inside. When we focus our attention on others, it can liberate us from feelings of anxiety and depression.

Community service, whether by volunteering, making reparations, or simply reaching out to those we've hurt, helps restore a sense of belonging and connection to the whole. By giving back to the community, we take responsibility for our actions and demonstrate our commitment to making a positive impact on the world. Acts of service can also help us regain trust, both from others and from ourselves. Even if we can't undo the harm we've caused, we can work to create something good from our mistakes.

Ultimately, engaging in community service allows us to shift our focus from self-blame to self-healing. It reminds us that we are part of a larger whole and that our actions, both good and bad, have a ripple effect on the lives of others. When we connect meaningfully with other people, we begin to heal the wounds of moral injury.

Maryanne emphasizes the importance of offering support to those who have caused unintentional harm to others. This support doesn't require forgiveness but recognizes the person's pain and reminds them they belong to the community or the human family. After Brian died, she reflected on a letter from a girl she had never met, expressing sympathy and inviting her to join a social activity. This was a small but powerful gesture of connection.

Maryanne concludes by urging us to consider how we might respond to those who have unintentionally caused harm to others. Rather than retreating, a simple act of connection can have a profoundly healing impact. Then, she returns to Apollo and Hyacinth, where Apollo created a beautiful flower from his tragic mistake. Unlike Apollo, humans cannot heal alone—we need each other to find meaning and repair the damage caused by our actions.

If you, like me, are moved by Maryann Jacobi Gray's experience with moral injury, check out her TEDx talk by following this link:

Maryann Jacobi Gray, It Hurts to Hurt Someone: https://tedx.ucla.edu/project/maryann_jacobi_gray_it_hurts_to_hurt_so	meone/

When discussing her experience with moral injury, Maryanne started with Apollo. If you are moved to discuss it, I hope you, like me, will begin with her. Hearing her speech touched me deeply and is a part of my healing journey.

Moral Injury, Guilt, and Shame

While Maryanne's speech provides a comprehensive analysis of moral injury, a few additional points are worth noting. First, we must clarify two words frequently used as synonyms: *guilt* and *shame*. Indeed, they are closely linked, but they differ in meaningful ways. Guilt typically arises when we believe we have done something wrong. It could be something as simple as stealing an apple from a store or as serious as infidelity.

We may feel guilty about an action and desire to keep it a secret. Shame, however, is more about feeling like we are fundamentally flawed because of what we've done, which leads to an overall sense of unworthiness. With guilt, we may still believe we are good at heart, but shame turns the dagger on our self-identity, making us feel rotten. Guilt can be "I did it," but shame convicts the soul as we tell ourselves, "I can't believe I did it."

Moral injury differs from both guilt and shame. It goes beyond feeling bad about one's action; it's about feeling like we have betrayed our essence. Feelings of deep regret, self-blame, and a sense of alienation from others often accompany the pain of moral injury. We may feel disconnected from our core values and, as a result, struggle with inner conflict, hopelessness, or a diminished sense of purpose.

As I have indicated, some people are overly conscientious. If you fall into this category, even the most innocent error may manifest as moral injury. It's inevitable because this personality has a poor sense of self-worth and feels compelled to adhere to the most stringent moral standards. For him, there is only right and wrong; no shades of grey exist. For such a person, moral injury can arise from various situations. Some common triggers may include:

- *Violence or Harm*: In Maryanne's case, she was involved in causing harm to someone through no fault of her own. Yet, the incident left her with deep psychological suffering that lasted a lifetime.

- *Betrayal or Dishonesty*: Engaging in deception or betraying someone's trust, especially in romantic relationships, may cause some individuals to experience moral injury. This could also involve the children of divorced parents, as we may feel we're supposed to protect or care for them. This phenomenon is also evident in professional environments, particularly in leadership roles. Some people, like me, are so sensitive that they may experience moral injury when harshly spoken to by a boss or subordinate.

- *Inaction or Failure to Intervene*: Sometimes, moral injury arises not from what we've done, but from what we've not done. Failing to intervene when we see harm occurring or when we have the power to prevent it can be just as damaging as direct involvement in causing harm.

Law enforcement is a classic example of where moral injury may occur. If a police officer is expected to uphold the shield by remaining silent when they witness abuse of power, they may experience moral injury. It may also occur in the military, sports organizations, or any closed-knit group where members are expected to close ranks in the face of controversy.

The list of situations where moral injury arises can be extensive. Beyond personal mistakes, moral injury can stem from external pressures, such as cultural or institutional demands that compel individuals to compromise their values and adopt a "groupthink" mentality. In addition to law enforcement and the military, it can also arise in corporate settings, healthcare, and sports teams, where authority or societal expectations may prompt individuals to act against their moral compass and align with the team.

The emotional fallout from such experiences can be profound. Individuals may feel overwhelmed by guilt, anger, sadness, and a sense of isolation. These emotions often lead to mental health struggles like anxiety, depression, and PTSD. In some cases, they can escalate into thoughts of suicide. The weight of moral injury can make it feel like there's no escape, especially when the person believes they cannot make amends or seek the support they need.

As we close, I invite you to reflect on what you gleaned from Maryanne's story. It answered several questions for me about why I suffered from divorce, which I will discuss in another chapter. From personal experience, there is no doubt that moral injury is a painful and complex emotional experience. Still, it is not one that you must face alone or without hope.

I've mentioned Dr. Abraham Low in this book, who famously said: "There are no hopeless cases. A patient may feel helpless, but they are not hopeless." By acknowledging the impact of your actions, working to forgive yourself, and taking concrete steps toward healing, you can begin to repair the damage caused by moral injury and discover that you are not hopeless.

Ultimately, healing from moral injury is about reclaiming your sense of integrity, your ability to live in alignment with your values, and your capacity to move forward with passion and self-compassion for yourself and others. The journey may be long, but it can lead to more profound wisdom, self-acceptance, and emotional resilience.

Worksheet

1. What is Moral Injury?
Definition Recap: Moral injury is the psychological distress that arises when our intentional or unintentional actions violate our beliefs about right and wrong. It often involves a profound internal conflict between our actions and our values, resulting in feelings of guilt, shame, and emotional distress.

Reflection:

1. Have you ever encountered a situation where your actions conflicted with your core values or ethical principles?

   Briefly describe the situation: _______________
   ____
   ____
   ____
   ____

2. How did you feel about yourself after the incident: ________________________________

____

____

____

____

3. Identifying Examples of Moral Injury: The chapter shares several examples of moral injury, ranging from tragic accidents to minor but emotionally significant situations.

   Reflect on the examples (e.g., Maryann's accident, the sober driver's moment of distraction, the soldier in combat, the divorce).

____

____

____

____

   Do any of these examples resonate with you?

   How do you relate to the emotional struggles of these individuals?

   Can you think of a situation in your own life that might involve moral injury? ___________

____

____

____

____

4. The Emotional Toll of Moral Injury

The chapter emphasizes that moral injury includes harm to others and damage to one's integrity and identity. This internal conflict can lead to profound emotional distress.

Reflect on how the emotional pain of moral injury manifests for you.

Do you experience shame, guilt, or self-recrimination when you believe you've caused harm? _______________________________________

____

____

____

How do these feelings impact your self-perception or your relationships with others?

____

____

____

____

5. Healing from Moral Injury: The Three Key Strategies

Maryann Jacobi Gray offers three key strategies for healing from moral injury: Accountability, Compassion, and Community Service.

Reflection:

Accountability (Acknowledge the Harm): Is there a situation where you could take more responsibility for the harm you caused? What would it take for you to acknowledge the harm? ______________________________

____

____

____

____

Compassion: (Showing Empathy for Yourself and Others.) Reflect on a time when you were particularly self-critical. What would it look like for you to extend compassion toward yourself during that time? How could you offer the same compassion to others who have wronged you? _________________

____

____

____

____

Community Service: (Reconnecting and Making Amends.) How might you begin to reconnect with others or make amends for the harm you've caused? _________________

____

____

____

What small acts of service or connection could you engage in to begin the healing process? _________________

____

____

____

____

6. The Role of Compassion in Healing Moral
Injury

Reflection: How do you practice self-compassion in your daily life? When faced with guilt or shame, what can you do to offer yourself grace and understanding? _________

____

____

____

____

How might your understanding of compassion influence your relationship with others who have harmed you? _________________

____

____

____

____

7. Exploring Maryann Jacobi Gray's Story: As I admit, Maryann Jacobi Gray's experience

with moral injury deeply impacted me. Her involvement in the tragic death of a child, despite not being at fault, caused significant emotional turmoil.

Reflection: How did Maryann's story resonate with you? Did it change how you think about their emotional struggles after unintentional harm? ______________________________

____
____
____
____

Have you ever experienced a moment of unintentional wrongdoing that still haunts you? Based on what you've learned from Maryann's story, what steps might you take toward healing? ______________________________

____
____
____
____

8. Clarifying guilt and shame: Guilt and shame are often used interchangeably, but are distinct emotions. This section will help you reflect on these differences.

Definition Recap: *Guilt*: Arises when you believe you've done something wrong. You may feel bad about a specific action, but consider yourself fundamentally sound.

Example: "I made a mistake, but I'm not bad."

Shame: A deep and pervasive feeling that you are fundamentally flawed. You feel that what you did reflects who you are at your core.

Example: "I am bad because of what I did."

____

____

____

____

Reflection: Can you recall a time when you felt guilty? What was the action or event that triggered this feeling? Did you still view yourself as a good person despite your guilt? Why or why not? _______________________

____

____

____

____

Can you recall a time when you felt shame? What was the situation, and how did it affect your self-identity or sense of worth? Did this feeling change how you saw yourself as a person? _______________________

____

____

____

____

9. Moving Forward: (Healing from Moral Injury) Healing from moral injury is a journey. It involves confronting the harm caused, practicing self-compassion, and reconnecting with others through service and making amends.

Action Plan: Write down a few steps to begin healing from a past moral injury. This could involve an act of accountability, a gesture of compassion for yourself, or a way to reconnect with your community or those you've hurt. ___

____

____

____

____

Closing Thought

It's essential to remember that healing from moral injury is not a quick or overnight process. It requires time, patience, and a willingness to confront your pain. You can begin the path toward emotional recovery and peace by acknowledging your feelings, practicing compassion, and re-engaging with your values.

Chapter 8

Marriage and Divorce

A few decades ago, during a personal transformation workshop, a facilitator known for her direct and confrontational approach, called me a "moron" in relationships. Indeed, I might have been immature and inexperienced, but I wasn't stupid. The insult stung, leaving a wound that lingered longer than I like to admit. Yet, despite the crude comment, I stayed with the course.

Looking back, I realize that my decision reflected my fragile emotional state. Someone with a strong sense of self-worth, who knew their value and had clear boundaries, might have walked out because of such a belittling comment. But I didn't leave, as I was trapped in a spiral of emotional distress. At that point in my life, I was drowning in anxiety, depression, and a profound sense of loneliness.

My inner world felt like a continuous storm I couldn't escape. The emotional pain I was experiencing was so overwhelming that I couldn't see through it, let alone recognize that

I deserved better treatment. From this place of turmoil and self-doubt, I continued to make some of the worst decisions of my life. I allowed others to define me, and I remained in toxic situations because, deep down, I didn't believe I was worthy of anything different.

Reflecting on my history, I now understand that my emotional state heavily influenced my decisions. It wasn't rational thinking or clarity that guided my life; instead, it was a desperate attempt to escape discomfort. This only deepened the relentless cycle of intense negativity, self-loathing, and self-sabotage.

Discussing relationships isn't easy for me, not just because of my past struggles but also because I've often failed to build the healthy and lasting connections I had longed for. As I look back on my journey through marriage and divorce, I want to focus on the lessons I've learned, the painful experiences that shaped my growth, and, most importantly, how I've come to understand myself through them.

However, before I dive into the complexities of my story, I want to share something important: I consider myself blessed in many ways. Despite being divorced, I have consistently attracted women of high character who have loved and cared for me. I still experience that love today and give it freely in return. Furthermore, I have warm feelings for every woman whose hand I've held, recognizing that each one has shaped me in meaningful ways and left me with many positive memories.

Given my hardships, I suspect this may surprise some readers, but it's true. In a strange twist of fate, I believe that many of my romantic partners would also have positive reflections about me. Of course, I'm not suggesting I would bat 100 here, but overall, given my circumstances, I think I did well amid emotional turmoil, and some of my friends would give me credit for that, knowing that I did not intend to disrupt their lives.

However, it's important to acknowledge reality: it's challenging to build an intimate life when you're drowning in anxiety and depression. It's hard to give your best when you feel at your worst. You can't express true love when you don't have it for yourself. The ways I entered and left relationships were often influenced by the patterns of an unhealthy mind clouded by fear, self-doubt, and emotional instability. Creating a healthy, lasting bond with another person is impossible when you're not well inside. It's like trying to build a house on sand. You may get something that resembles a foundation, but it won't hold up when the storms come. And the storms always come.

Looking back, it's abundantly clear that the emotional toll of failed relationships was not just about the love I lost but the opportunity to know and love myself honestly. Every breakup, every divorce, was an invitation to heal, to grow, and to *break free* from the patterns that had kept me stuck for so long. It took time, but I eventually learned that the key to a fulfilling relationship is not finding the perfect partner but becoming a whole, healthy person first. Only then can we show up as our true, vulnerable, strong, and healthy selves, ready to give love without expectation.

Before I delve deeper into my journey, I want to address one more thing. This isn't a space for petty self-disclosures or sensationalism. Such an approach not only detracts from the purpose of this book. I'm also mindful that sharing my journey in a book may reach many people, including my children, past partners, and their families and friends. So, let me set this intention from the outset: this chapter is about my story, my path, and the lessons I've learned. It is not a platform for gossiping or airing details about anyone else, past or present. The focus here is on me, not those who have shared parts of their lives with me. With that in mind, I invite you to join me as I share my story.

The Effects of Poor Self-Esteem

If you've been following along in this book, you've likely noticed that I've touched on my struggles with low self-esteem and limited confidence. What I haven't yet explored in depth is how these issues took root in my life—and how they shaped much of my emotional distress. I can't pinpoint exactly where it all began, but I didn't see myself as capable for much of my early years. I was afraid of the dark, nervous about public speaking, and anxious about attending social gatherings.

This wasn't always the case, though. As a child, I had a strong sense of self and believed in my abilities. I was a Sunday School scholar at my church and enjoyed standing before others to share the day's lesson. I knew I could learn quickly and had an easy time grasping new concepts.

Before I was even 10, one of my teachers described me as "superlative." I learned the symbols for many elements on the periodic table. I could recite all 46 counties in my state alphabetically by sixth grade. I even wrote a letter to a local television station before I turned 14, advocating for fair treatment of all people, regardless of their skin color.

By age 16, I had gravitated toward the civil rights movement, a pivotal moment that shaped my understanding of justice and equality. I participated in local demonstrations, attended a Congress of Racial Equality (CORE) convention, and actively fought to include Black Studies in our high school curriculum. These were bold actions for someone my age, reflecting the ambition and confidence of a young person who believed in his ability to make a difference.

But despite all of this—despite the evidence of my capabilities and ambition—I never truly felt like I was "good enough." It was a paradox I struggled to understand: how could

I be so driven and capable yet feel so small inside? This disconnect between what I could do and how I felt about myself created a deepseated insecurity that would follow me into adulthood, especially in my relationships. For years, I silently battled the damaging effects of poor self-esteem, unaware of how profoundly it influenced my decisions and emotional life.

Like many of you, I had a supportive network of teachers in my early years. However, there were moments when their feedback sowed seeds of doubt about my worth. One such moment occurred in elementary school when my English teacher praised the content of my essay but criticized my handwriting, deeming it too poor to be displayed on the bulletin board.

At the time, I accepted her judgment without much thought. But looking back, I realize how deeply that experience affected me. It wasn't just about my handwriting—it was about how her words made me feel like I wasn't good enough, or that my best effort could still be dismissed because it didn't meet some arbitrary standard. What lingered with me over the years was not the essay itself but the emotional

272

residue of that rejection. I now understand that these experiences can imprint our sense of self, especially in our formative years.

According to Michael Singer, these experiences become energies that can be trapped within us if we don't process them. He explains that when we fail to release these negative energies fully, they remain lodged in our psyche, subtly influencing how we perceive ourselves and interact with the world.

During my junior year of high school, a remark from an administrator also left a lasting negative mark on me, one that I would carry for years. At the time, I was deeply involved in the local civil rights movement, actively participating in protests at my high school and organizing to add Black Studies to the curriculum.

Alongside my peers, I marched and fought for equality, hoping to make a tangible difference. But despite my involvement in such meaningful work, which I believed was rooted in justice and progress, the administrator pulled me aside one day and offered a suggestion that still stings in my memory. He told me that since

I was good in band, I would be better off leaving school and joining the armed forces, specifically the military band.

I remember pausing, uncertain. Was he suggesting I enlist after graduation? But his implication was clear: he didn't think I would likely finish high school and wanted to get rid of me. In his eyes, my best future lay on a path removed from academic or professional aspirations, just a young person whose value could be reduced to a place in a military band.

I couldn't fully comprehend the weight of his words or the subtle message they conveyed. Looking back, however, I realize that this moment planted another seed of doubt in me, which would continue to grow over the years, slowly suffocating my self-belief.

Though I fought for justice and equality, his words told me something different: I wasn't worthy of a bright or expansive future. I began to internalize that I wasn't good enough, that no matter how hard I worked, it might never be enough. This doubt also affected my relationships with my peers and teachers, as I wondered whether they saw me the same way. I started to question whether I could achieve anything significant.

There were many other verbal wounds I internalized during my early years. Still, one from a minister at my church cut deeply. He believed his role was to maintain peace in the community, no matter the cost. This meant silencing anyone who challenged the status quo, including young civil rights advocates.

One Sunday, with no regard for my presence in the congregation, he publicly labeled me a troublemaker, saying I would never amount to anything. After all these years, I still don't fully understand why he said that about me—perhaps it was simply because he was doing what those in power had instructed him to do. I know his words stuck with me, festering in many ways I couldn't fully comprehend at the time. Strangely, though, I never came to hate him.

Years later, after earning my doctorate, I visited his home. For reasons I can only trace back to my high school days and the guilt he might have felt, he struggled to look me in the eye. It was a stark reminder of the lasting effects of verbal abuse, which can shape a person for years to come. However, it's important to note that I have also found healing and growth through self-reflection and therapy, and I continue to work on myself to overcome the adverse effects of these experiences.

The emotional knot created by those words and assumptions never unravels quickly. As Singer suggests, when negative experiences like these go unaddressed, they can shape our identity in ways that deeply impact our sense of self-worth. For years, I carried the burden of that doubt, which gnawed at my confidence and sense of possibility. It was as though I had internalized the notion that failure was inevitable and that my best efforts would always fall short. It wasn't just a matter of underestimating my potential in those moments; it became the lens through which I saw my entire life.

The seeds of low self-esteem had been planted, and it took me years of reflection and healing to untangle them. However, through this process, I discovered the power of self-reflection and the healing that comes with it, which inspired me to share my story and offer hope to others struggling with similar experiences.

College Education

Many of my high school classmates attended universities in our state. Still, none of my high school teachers seemed to believe I could reach that level. And they offered no guidance or advice on selecting a college. I started at a small institution, one that even a fellow high school graduate mocked as another high school. But I'm grateful for my college because it set me on the path to higher education, and it's where I began to see myself in a more positive light.

Some professors treated me as though I had the potential to achieve great things. For example, my botany professor told me I belonged at the university. Other instructors praised my reading skills and considered me an above-average student. My French teacher even pointed to me as a positive example for my peers, telling them that if I could learn French, so could they. One history professor had so much confidence in me that he entrusted me with teaching his class whenever he was absent.

Despite the academic success of my undergraduate years, I remained the country boy who didn't fully recognize my worth. I recall the nights I questioned my adequacy and place in the academic world. I was allowed to grow intellectually, but emotionally, I remained stunted. I earned good grades in college, yet I still couldn't convince myself I was enough. I didn't know myself—I only knew the stories others had about me. When I stepped into an elite university for my master's degree, I was bombarded with narratives about my lack of preparation, which only fueled my self-doubt.

Graduate school was a battleground for my self-esteem. A professor who believed in my intellectual capacity for doctoral work also thought my undergraduate education lacked rigor. He even suggested that I could succeed at an Ivy League school. But he added this condition: I would also need to take a freshman-level writing course if he recommended me for doctoral studies. His words were like a sledgehammer to my confidence. I felt like I had wasted years pursuing an education only to be told I wasn't good enough. Instead of encouragement, I received criticism about my writing abilities.

It took me a long time to recognize my value as a professional. It wasn't until I started filming courses for distance education in the 1990s that I began to see my strengths. I had never seen myself as a teacher before, and no one had ever pointed out that I was a natural communicator. Watching my lessons made me realize that I spoke passionately as if I truly loved what I was doing and cared about my students. I liked the texture of my voice and how easily I could organize information. No one had helped me see that I had many talents beyond my academic struggles.

But by then, the damage had been done. I never learned to believe in myself. It's funny now, but when I started teaching at a college at 23, one of my students even encouraged me to believe in myself. Learning to see myself as capable and worthy has been a gradual process. Despite publishing books and articles and devoting myself entirely to my profession, I still couldn't see myself as worthwhile. And the faculty and students around me reflected the image I saw in the mirror.

The Apostolic Church

By the time I was 23, I was a complete emotional wreck. I wanted to be emotionally healthy, I honestly did, but I couldn't seem to find a way out of the melancholy that haunted me. My anxiety and depression were suffocating, and I was desperately seeking something to make sense of the chaos inside my mind. I knew I needed help, and that's when someone mentioned a unique church to me.

While I had been around churches my entire life, I had never heard of an Apostolic Church. In desperation and despair, I decided to turn my life over to God and the church. It seemed like the answer at the time—finally, an opportunity for renewal, a fresh start, and surrendering myself so God could make things right.

Initially, turning to the church seemed like a positive step. However, instead of finding the lasting peace I yearned for, my anxiety and depression only deepened. The church, which was meant to be a sanctuary, became all-consuming. Many of us were seeking something—some for freedom from addiction, others, like me, from the crushing weight of mental illness. I had hoped that faith would be the answer. But I was seeking solace in the wrong place, using it as a crutch instead of confronting the issues within myself.

Looking back, I now understand that the church wasn't the issue. The real problem was I turned the church into my escape, my sanctuary, and perhaps even my cult. What I truly needed was professional care, therapy, and someone trained to help me unravel the tangled mess in my mind. But in those days, therapy was a foreign concept, especially for a rural kid from the black community. I was too lost to seek it out, and no one extended a helping hand. So, I turned to the church, hoping it would provide the healing I so desperately needed.

However, the church wasn't equipped to provide the emotional help I required. Instead, it only reinforced my self-loathing. The leadership, while well-meaning, often made me feel inadequate. One leader told me I wasn't "suitable" to be a Sunday School superintendent, even though I was more than capable of teaching there since it was my profession. (This is hilarious to me today because I went on to become the inaugural director of an academic program, designing curricula, hiring faculty, and managing a budget.) I was devastated because I shared that minister's low impression of myself back then.

At that moment, the weight of every negative comment I'd heard about myself rushed back, flooding my thoughts. It wasn't just about the position; it was about the message I internalized—that I wasn't good enough, that I would never be good enough. Furthermore, that church leader was the first to be bold enough to tell me something was wrong with me. He prayed for me, but his comments caused more harm than good.

This constant cycle of self-doubt and unrelenting criticism eventually took its toll. I questioned my worth, purpose, and place in the world. The church that had promised salvation only seemed to amplify my internal chaos. I kept pushing myself, trying to prove something to others, trying to fit into a mold that didn't align with who I was. I couldn't escape the feeling that I always fell short, no matter how hard I tried. After four long years in that church, I experienced burnout, a state of mental, physical, and emotional exhaustion. I couldn't keep up the façade any longer.

I can vividly remember sitting in that congregation as a scripture from a letter from Apostle Paul to the Corinthian church seeped into my mind: *There is a great door opening for you, but there are many adversaries.* My soul immediately said I had to go. Walking away from the church felt like I had failed in many ways, but it was also the only way I could start to reclaim some control over my life. I didn't have all the answers, but I knew I couldn't stay there and continue to spiral into a deeper state of emotional dysfunction.

It wasn't easy. Leaving meant losing a community that, in some ways, had become my entire world. But in the end, I realized that I needed to *break free* from the false promises I had built around my faith to heal. I needed to face myself, and for the first time, I acknowledged that I couldn't do it alone. Soon after leaving the church, a great door opened, just as the scripture had said. I received a call from an associate dean at a university, who offered me a teaching fellowship to pursue my doctoral degree. That call changed my life, and I entered a profession at a level I thought was beyond my reach.

Anxiety, Depression, Marriage

Many of us made life-altering decisions in church. Some young people had many children, just as women had done in the mid-twentieth century. Some women had ten or more kids by the time they reached their thirties. The church was the place where you got married and started a family! We were all people of God and mostly good-natured.

Getting married wasn't inherently a bad idea for me. I was already 25, but I was not prepared for marriage emotionally. The internal turmoil I had been battling for so long quickly began to seep into my marriage. This turbulence created overwhelming tension in my family, which I couldn't escape. The weight of my constant self-doubt and criticism, coupled with the lingering anxiety and depression, was slowly eroding the very foundation of what was supposed to be a partnership built on love and trust.

Undoubtedly, I expected my poor spouse to have the answers, but if I didn't, she surely would not have them. My wife at the time, though supportive as much as possible, couldn't fully understand the depth of my emotional pain. I struggled to communicate what was happening inside me, and when I did, it felt as though I was pushing her away even more. The more I tried to "fix" myself to be the person I thought I should be, the more disconnected I became from the person I was supposed to be for my partner. It became an endless cycle of highs and lows.

Every interaction felt like an emotional battleground, with me fighting to keep my head above water while simultaneously holding on to the belief that I could somehow be enough. But no matter how much I tried, my sense of inadequacy only deepened. I began to wonder if the problems in my marriage were reflections of my brokenness, an indication that I was too damaged to be loved or understood. The anxiety weighed on me heavily, making every day feel like a struggle to get through, let alone thrive.

I began questioning everything—my marriage, my role as a partner, and even my self-worth. Was I failing in all aspects of my life, or was I seeing myself through distorted lenses? With every passing day, the line between my mental health and my relationship blurred, and I could no longer separate the two. The psychological distress I felt wasn't just internal—it was now affecting my family. Getting married with episodes of clinical depression is one of the worst things anyone could do. This inevitably takes a toll on a marriage and can lead to divorce.

Nevertheless, my wife and I hung in there for almost three decades of marriage. Because of its duration, the marriage was not a failure. We also had three children and suffered the death of one of them as a couple. Our remaining children are thriving and productive citizens; both are college-educated and hold graduate degrees, including a doctorate. They own their homes and financially support themselves on their journey through life. From the outside, our marriage looked perfect. Still, on the inside,

I fought an emotional war, and I was determined to see if I could resolve it.

In fighting for my life, I made a few critical mistakes that led me down the path of divorce. The first one is that I sought advice from other people. Second, I took a job far away and started building a new life. It was not all bad, even though I felt strong emotions about losing my family early on. However, my experience was exhilarating; for the first time, I began to experience boundless happiness. I remember sharing my feelings with a family member who said she wanted some of my joy.

My contentment was evident, and I distinctly remember sitting in a program for honor students when the professor giving the talk singled me out, telling the audience that I was someone who loved his work. He had seen me around campus and noticed the glimmer in my eyes and how I beamed like a bright light. I had been teaching for almost thirty years, and no one had ever said such a nice thing about me. I had achieved everything I had prayed for.

Then, I made the mistake of starting a relationship before I was ready. I was not prepared for the whirlwind of anger, bitterness, and criticisms that came my way. It launched me into another round of anxiety, depression, and despair.

Marriage and Divorce

Divorce was one of the most emotionally charged experiences in my life. It's a topic I have shied away from openly discussing. As I reflected on moral injury in Chapter 7, divorce, for me, stirred profound feelings of guilt and an overwhelming sense that I had caused pain to those I loved.

This feeling of moral injury, however, is not universal. Some people seem to find peace or even joy in their divorces. I've heard others say, "Divorce was the best thing that ever happened to me," or claim to be "happily divorced," almost as if divorce itself can be a liberating event. Some even use the phrase "I've been well married," meaning they've navigated multiple marriages and, in their view, found a sense of fulfillment or peace in each one.

But for me, divorce wasn't a path to peace at all. It was an emotional earthquake that shattered the life I had imagined for myself. The pain wasn't just about the end of a marriage but about the dissonance between the life I had hoped for and the reality I had created. It's a torment that pushes you to confront the depths of who you are and what you've done.

When you're caught in the emotional storm of divorce, it's essential to step back and slow down. I have often said that you must stop completely when you're lost in confusion. It's never wise to make life-changing decisions in chronic stress. The impulse to push through the pain, to continue moving forward as if nothing is wrong, can be overpowering.

As my confusion deepened, I pushed forward, ignoring the emotional storm within me. Some people can quickly weather rapid changes, but it was too much for me, and I imploded. Further, I was unprepared for the judgment and silent stares of those around me. The people I thought were friendly to me walked away as if I had a contagious disease.

Life is full of many twists and turns—it's simply its nature. However, one truth remains: *a new life cannot begin until the old one has ended.* We must allow the dust to settle before stepping into a new relationship, especially after a long marriage. If we don't, life has a way of teaching this lesson through painful experiences.

Everything has a purpose. Divorce, although agonizing, serves a purpose. Perhaps it's meant to teach us, forcing us to grow emotionally and spiritually. Over the years, I've spoken to many people about their experiences, and their stories reveal just how complex life after marriage can be.

One man told me his ex-wife remarried quickly, yet they continued their intimate relationship. Another father had children with his ex-wife and his new wife in the same year. A woman once confided in me on a long flight that she had a child with her ex-husband's cousin. Her family had ostracized her, and she struggled to find her place.

Some people remarry the same day their divorce is finalized, while others later discover they had never actually divorced in the first place. Many navigate these emotional transitions with resilience. But for those who carry deep wounds—what I referred to in Chapter 7 as "moral injury"—divorce can be devastating. I know this because I am one of those people.

Why am I sharing these deeply personal details about my life? Because I know the pain of multiple divorces, and I don't believe anyone should suffer alone. If my story can help even one person navigate their emotional struggles, my experiences—my mistakes and choices—will not have been in vain. I have been married four times to three women—twice to the same one. After divorcing my children's mother, I rushed into another marriage just six months later.

My decisions bewildered my adult children and my ex-wife. Their pain was visible, and witnessing their hurt made my emotional state even more fragile. I felt out of control, terrified that I was losing my mental balance. My sister and a close friend urged me to seek professional help, a suggestion that became a turning point.

Therapy and medication followed, but they only scratched the surface of my pain. Someone close to me feared I would mentally collapse under the weight of it all. Sometimes, it felt like my mind might slip away entirely, and my only goal was survival.

Desperate to relieve my emotional storm, I turned to books, teachings, and philosophies that promised psychological healing. But nothing could instantly stop the *tsunami* inside me. I had to endure it. What hurt most was how others responded to my struggles. I had hoped for empathy, but instead, I often felt judged and isolated—just as I had in the 1980s. The connections I so desperately needed seemed to vanish, leaving me alone with my pain.

The more isolated I became, the more I internalized the belief that I had failed again—that I had "done marriage wrong" once more. I thought the only way to fix what I had broken was to start over. But my struggle had nothing to do with the marriage itself. *The divorce stemmed from a mind that believed it could go back and repair the damage. But you can never go back. The past is gone.* It was my unresolved pain that continued to follow me.

Indeed, falling in love is intoxicating. After everything I had been through, I remained open to marriage. I met someone new, and our relationship moved quickly. None of the entanglements I had before existed. Red flags warned us to slow down, but we ignored them all. I wanted to be married, and this relationship felt more right than wrong. My heart pounded with excitement as I stepped into a new chapter. I believed I was starting from a "pure place." We were married six months later.

But looking back, I see now that I was not emotionally well. Anxiety and depression —my old shadow—soon crept back in. Despite therapy, medication, and my best efforts, the pain inside me remained too deep for any quick fix. As my professional life unraveled for reasons I struggled to comprehend, I retired at 65. My marriage ended soon after. These were my choices, and I take full responsibility for them. If sharing my journey brings comfort or clarity to someone else, then the struggles I faced will have served a purpose.

The emotional toll of my divorce was immense. The feelings of moral injury and fractured self-esteem almost consumed me. I never imagined I would be someone with multiple wives, and yet, here I was, grappling with the very reality that I had once hoped to avoid. The emotional pain was not just about the loss of a relationship but also about the loss of a part of myself. The oneness once so powerful left an emotional void when it was broken, a void that seemed impossible to fill.

Some may struggle to understand how I can still believe in marriage despite my history. But I do. The Scriptures say, "Two shall become one," and I have experienced the truth of that statement. This isn't merely a spiritual or religious ideal—it speaks to a profound truth about the nature of intimacy. When two people come together in a shared life, something mysterious and deeply emotional happens. And when that bond is severed, the pain is intense. You feel not only the loss of a relationship but the loss of a part of yourself. That oneness, once so powerful, leaves an emotional void when it's broken. This belief in the profound truth of intimacy is what made the pain of divorce so intense for me.

Of course, every relationship is different, and the healing journey is uniquely personal. But for me, the process of untangling the bond of a marriage, of facing that deep, emotional void, has been one of the most challenging experiences of my life. The agony of separation, of losing that shared existence, is something no one can truly prepare for.

While divorce is undoubtedly painful, it's also true that not all relationships are meant to last forever. Life's challenges—whether they're illness, addiction, infidelity, or simply growing apart—can place unbearable strains on even the strongest unions. Scripture acknowledges this, recognizing that divorce may be a necessary path when forgiveness becomes too difficult, particularly in cases of infidelity or severe betrayal. Divorce, while not ideal, is acknowledged as a possible solution when reconciliation feels impossible.

Some marriages survive these challenges, but for many, it's essential to recognize when it's time to rebuild or when it may be healthier to part ways. It's always better to work through difficulties together if you're willing. However, when forgiveness becomes unachievable, sometimes the only choice is to let go.

The road to healing is not linear; no matter how often you've been through it, you are always learning. My journey with love, marriage, and emotional healing continues. I've learned that healing is a process, and taking time is okay. I've learned a few valuable lessons from my multiple divorces, which I offer for your consideration.

Reflections of a Divorcee

My relationships and hardships taught me valuable lessons that may help others navigate marriage and divorce. I acknowledge that my past experiences shaped my perspectives. Still, I share it in the hope that it might offer insights to anyone open to hearing it:

- *Dating and Marriage*: Some people meet and marry quickly, building lasting and meaningful relationships. While there is no one-size-fits-all approach, taking the time to consider marriage before committing can be beneficial. Discuss your hopes, dreams, and expectations for the relationship with your partner before making such a significant and potentially permanent decision. When difficulties arise, it's easier to lean on these shared values and aspirations to guide you through tough times so you can return to love.
- *Togetherness*: Marriage, or any committed relationship, involves two people. Keep your marriage separate from the rest of your personal life, including your relationship with your ex. No one outside your relationship can honestly know what's best for you. Well-meaning friends and family often offer advice that reflects their needs and desires, rather than what's best for your relationship.

It's essential to maintain an open and intimate line of communication between the two of you and work together toward solutions. Furthermore, if you seek counseling, consider doing it together—as a couple. Individual counseling for marriage problems may further strain the relationship.

- *Divorce and Abuse*: If you find yourself in an abusive situation—whether mental, emotional, or physical—prioritize your safety. Leave the problem as quickly as possible and seek support from trusted professionals and loved ones. Never stay in a relationship that threatens your physical safety.

- *Grieving the Divorce*: Divorce often feels like losing a part of yourself. It's like death. Many people who have been married may not want to face being alone again. But it's crucial not to rush into another relationship in an attempt to fill the void. The grief that comes with the end of a marriage is real and needs to be processed. Take the time you need to mourn the loss and heal emotionally before opening your heart to someone else.

Regarding divorce itself, consider these additional points:

- *Don't seek advice about your marriage*: No one outside your marriage can determine if you should divorce. Trust your instincts and make choices based on what's right for you and your partner, not because of external pressure.
- *Create a Divorce Agreement*: It's best to approach the divorce decision as you did with marriage—do it together. If divorce is inevitable, approach the process with mutual respect. Both partners deserve to be heard, and it's essential to reach an agreement that acknowledges the end of the marriage while maintaining dignity and respect for one another.
- *Avoid starting another relationship too soon*: It's tempting to seek comfort after the end of a marriage, but rushing into another relationship can hinder genuine healing. Take time to process your emotions fully before moving forward.

Insights from Therapists

Healing from divorce is a complex process that requires both time and self-reflection. Marriage and family therapists emphasize the importance of taking this time to understand oneself and navigate the emotional aftermath. Dr. John Gottman, a renowned researcher in marital stability, emphasizes that successful relationships are founded on emotional awareness and effective conflict resolution. When communication breaks down irreparably, or when one or both partners are unable to meet each other's needs, divorce can sometimes be the healthiest decision, despite the pain it brings.

From my experience, feeling pain is inevitable. My emotions were all over the place, reeling from feelings of self-loathing and recrimination, anger, and depression. If possible, don't go through divorce alone, just as you wouldn't handle the death of a loved one alone. Join a support group or form one if none exists. You need to heal, and I offer these four practical tips to help you along the way as you navigate what may feel like an emotional roller-coaster in the aftermath of divorce:

- *Practice Mindfulness*: Take time to sit with your emotions without judgment. Allow yourself to feel, but also remind yourself that it's normal to experience a wide range of emotions during this transition.

- *Reframe Negative Thoughts*: Grab your pencil and paper, practice identifying negative thought patterns, such as blaming yourself or your ex, and replace them with more balanced perspectives. For example, instead of thinking, *"I failed at this marriage,"* try, *"I did the best I could, and now I have the opportunity to learn and grow from the experience."*

- *Cultivate Self-Compassion*: Treat yourself with the same kindness and understanding you would extend to a friend in a similar situation. Avoid harsh self-criticism and recognize that you are in the process of healing.

- *Focus on Self-Care*: Engage in activities that nurture your physical, emotional, and mental health. Exercise regularly, eat well, and engage in hobbies or activities that bring you joy and fulfillment. This will help you rebuild your sense of self and create a new foundation for your future.

Moreover, mental health professionals point out that many individuals experience significant personal growth and fulfillment after divorce. This journey is often marked by hope and the promise of a brighter future. Although it will take time, the rewards are well worth it.

As Dr. Harriet Lerner, a psychologist and relationship expert, wisely notes, "The journey of healing is not about moving on from your former spouse but about finding a sense of wholeness within yourself."

It's crucial to remember that divorce affects not only you and your spouse, but also their family and friends. Children, regardless of age, are deeply impacted by divorce. Acknowledging their feelings and experiences is crucial to help them navigate the transition in a healthy manner.

Older children may direct anger toward the parent they perceive as responsible and feel they are losing the stability and safety their family once provided. Younger children may face the challenge of adjusting to life in two homes and coping with the new people their parents bring into their lives. While I'm not here to make a value judgment on these experiences, it's essential to acknowledge that young children, even though they did not cause the breakup, may internalize the situation in ways that could profoundly affect them, including believing they were at fault.

Additionally, many overlook the impact of divorce on their extended family, particularly in-laws. While some may dismiss the importance of these relationships, especially if they feel distant, it's essential to consider the feelings of your in-laws, especially if you have a close bond with them. Divorce affects not only the couple but also those connected to them, even if they didn't initiate it. Furthermore, be mindful of their emotional journey, as maintaining a healthy relationship with them can benefit all parties involved.

There's one more important consideration: while your former spouse is not your enemy, you must be cautious about how and when you involve them in your new life. You can't serve two masters, and until you've established clear, healthy boundaries with your ex, it's best not to seek advice or engage in deep personal matters with them.

Over time, it may be possible to develop a friendship again, especially if you have children in common. However, remember that your emotional well-being is paramount. Don't put yourself in the middle of conflicting loyalties. Allowing this dynamic to persist can create unnecessary stress and sabotage your healing process. Protect your peace by maintaining clear boundaries; your well-being depends on it.

Finally, while divorce is undeniably emotionally painful, it can also be an opportunity for profound personal growth, self-discovery, and the possibility of a healthier future—whether that future includes another romantic relationship. This journey of healing and self-compassion can inspire you to emerge more substantial, with a deeper understanding of who you are and what you genuinely need for fulfillment. My divorce was intertwined with my mental health disorder, and my healing is intermixed with becoming healthy and whole.

Worksheet

If you're in a marriage or a relationship where you're experiencing abuse and have safety concerns, find a safe place and seek help. If you're in marriage counseling, do it with your spouse. Never pursue therapy alone if married unless, again, there are concerns for your safety. If a therapist recommends divorce when violence or infidelity are not issues, get another therapist. With that said, consider these points:

1. Reflect on the Issues with your spouse:

   - Action: Both partners individually list the top 3 issues in the relationship that contribute to feelings of dissatisfaction.

   - Prompt: Are these issues temporary, or do they reflect deeper, long-term concerns? Are they something you feel willing or able to work on together?

Free write: ________________________

____

____

____

____

2. Open Communication with your spouse:

   Action: Set aside 30 minutes to discuss your feelings openly and honestly without interruptions. Focus on "I" statements instead of blaming (e.g., "I feel..." vs "You always..."). Prompt: What underlying emotions (e.g., sadness, frustration, fear) contribute to the issues you're facing? _______________

____

____

____

____

____

____

3. Seek Therapy:

   Action: Explore the option of couples therapy or marriage counseling. Therapy can provide a neutral space for working through communication problems and emotional disconnects.

Prompt: Are both of you open to seeking professional help? What are your hopes or expectations for therapy?

Free write: _______________________________

____

____

____

4. Assess the Role of Intimacy:

Action: Reflect on the physical and emotional intimacy in your relationship. Consider how often you connect in meaningful ways.

Prompt: How can you improve or reignite intimacy in your relationship? Is there something missing or neglected that you both value?

Free write: _______________________________

____

____

____

5. Create a "Time-Out" Period when conversations become strained but don't shut down. That is, don't give each other the "silent treatment," which can be abusive:

Action: Agree to take a short "time-out" from major decisions for 1-2 weeks. Use this time for personal reflection, individual therapy, or a brief trial of living apart if necessary.
Prompt: How do you each feel after taking a step back? Do you feel more clarity about your relationship, or does the desire to separate feel stronger?

Free write: ___________________________
____
____
____
____

Decide to divorce or stay married, together.

Prompt: Do you both see a path to reconciliation, or do the issues feel insurmountable? How can you honor each other's needs, whether working together or parting ways?

____

____

____

____

6. Final Reflections: If children are involved, try to remain friends with clear boundaries. You may wish to remain friends if children are not involved, but it's essential to maintain clear boundaries.

Free write: _______________________________

____

____

____

____

Chapter 9

Your Spiritual Life

We are all bound to the throne of the Supreme Being by a flexible chain which restrains without enslaving us. The most wonderful aspect of the universal scheme of things is the action of free beings under divine guidance. Joseph de Maistre

Life is a profound mystery that everyone should recognize in some way. We fight, love, condemn, and forgive. Yet, regardless of what we do to one another, we all face the same unalterable truth: our existence in this world is finite. Every boy, girl, man, and woman knows that one day, we will leave this earthly plane.

What departs, however, is not the physical body. Across cultures and histories, humanity has crafted countless stories to make sense of what happens beyond the threshold of death. Some call it "the end," while others consider it a continuation—a transformation within the broader tapestry of existence. For many, this transition is labeled "death," while others see it as just another chapter in "life as we know it." Religions often offer interpretations: some promise heaven or warn of hell; others envision paradise or reincarnation. Despite the varied details, one constant remains: we all share a profound sense of mystery, a deep curiosity about what happens when the body ceases to function. This shared sense of mystery invites us to explore the idea of a Supreme Being—a force greater than ourselves, known by countless names across cultures.

Furthermore, the mystery that unites us is itself a wonder. The certainty of life and death, as we know it, and the eternal questions have humbled and inspired humanity for centuries, igniting our curiosity and prompting us to seek a deeper understanding. This chapter is not meant to debate the validity of any one religion or spiritual tradition.

Instead, it invites us to consider the existence of a Supreme Being, a concept that transcends specific religious beliefs. This Being, often referred to as God, the Universe, or the Divine, is a force that many believe cares for all forms of life—human, animal, plant, and even the seemingly inanimate, like rocks and rivers. Therefore, embracing this perspective means recognizing that we are supported and connected, no matter what unfolds in our personal lives or on our planet.

What happens when your body completes its physical journey? I cannot say know, and the question is not the purpose of this discussion. However, I am persuaded that our essence, that unique and universal part of ourselves, will ultimately merge with the infinite, with All That Is. This understanding transcends religious boundaries, and it is what I refer to as spirituality.

Nature's God

The United States of America was born in 1776 when the colonies declared independence from Great Britain. The first two paragraphs of the Declaration of Independence are profoundly practical, invoking common sense to explain why they took the extraordinary step of severing ties with the Mother Country. Their reasoning, however, was also deeply spiritual. In asserting their right to independence, they invoked the "Laws of Nature and of Nature's God."

They did not attempt to prove the existence of a Creator; instead, they stated the self-evident truth that God *is*. This declaration carries a weight that cannot be ignored. From this premise, they argued, it follows that all sentient beings are endowed with "unalienable rights"—rights that cannot be taken away except by their consent.

For the Founding Fathers, the belief that our rights and privileges are "endowed by their Creator" was not up for debate; it was a fundamental truth. This belief was not just a matter of faith but a practical understanding of human rights. Given this, it was logical that they had the right to establish a government that would respect and protect human rights.

Just as the Founding Fathers used common sense to explain the spiritual foundations of the United States, I will apply that same reasoning to affirm the concept of "Nature's God"—the Creator who *is*—a concept deeply rooted in all religious and spiritual traditions. Let's use some common sense to evaluate this proposition.

Every positive function within your body occurs automatically without your conscious control. Take, for example, your birth: Were you the cause of your existence? While the biological process can be understood in medical and scientific terms, a mystery remains. You didn't "will" yourself into existence. Neither did you choose the moment of your birth.

Moreover, your body functions independently of your conscious intent or thought, which is a humbling realization. Your heart pumps consistently, keeping you alive, and the breath you take is instinctual. You consume food, drink, breathe air, and expel waste, all of which sustain your life. These functions continue without your direct involvement. You created none of this. It was given to you. Your life, therefore, is a gift from this mystery, which, for millennia, many clergy and philosophers have sought to explain.

Therefore, biology reveals an undeniable truth: we do not make or control ourselves. While science can explain many aspects of our physical existence, it cannot account for the larger mystery of why we are here or the greater forces that govern our being. This mystery points toward a truth beyond our complete comprehension, but one that we are undeniably a part of. This, in essence, is the nature of the Creator—of "Nature's God."

The physical earth tells us the same thing. All foods are available, and the soil enables us to plant seeds and grow various vegetables and fruits. I don't want to start fighting with people who follow a wholefood-plant-based nutrition regimen, but we can find food in the sea and countless animals that roam the earth to nourish us.

Minerals in the earth can be used for heat, building structures, and fueling a technological revolution. We also draw from the earth's ores for our technologies and infrastructure. We don't need a geologist to tell us that minerals at the Earth's core are here for our benefit. We did not put them here; we discovered them with the genius given to humanity. There is something special about humans, but we didn't endow ourselves with this quality. As scripture says, *God made humans a little lower than the angels and crowned them with glory and honor.*

Humanity's intelligence reminds us of our innate genius, freely given. A glance at civilization demonstrates humanity's capacity to thrive. Medicine, as imperfect as it is, saves lives and improves the quality of life. Technology enables practitioners to examine the body, repair malfunctioning parts, and replace them with prosthetic components such as titanium knees and hips. The list of innovations we have is endless.

What's the point? Whether you are a believer or a nonbeliever, you are not doing any of this. Everything, including the earth, is freely given to us. Here's why this understanding is relevant for this chapter. To *break free* from emotional distress and achieve well-being, it's essential to acknowledge that a caring Supreme power is watching over you.

People acknowledge the Supreme in different ways. I'm not opening Pandora's box about the right path for you or anyone else. I will defer that debate to philosophers and theologians. What's important here is that you find the right path for you. You need to know this for yourself. You should search your heart and understand that the Supreme cares for you. You must take this stand and become immovable. The only way to enter the Kingdom of God is within you, and you need to uncover it.

Trust in the Supreme

As I've mentioned, I come from a Christian background. My spiritual journey began in the United Methodist Church, which shaped my understanding of God for much of my life. In my 24th year, I became deeply immersed in the doctrines of the Apostolic Church, which taught that salvation was exclusive to those who adhered to its belief system.

However, by my 28th year, I began questioning this exclusivity and gradually embraced a broader perspective that included all religions, finding value in their teachings and practices. This inclusive belief system served me well for many years. Although I distanced myself from the church, its teachings and traditions always came back to me.

After leaving the Apostolic Church, I no longer identified as religious. I neither advocate nor condemn any specific spiritual path. However, despite my departure from organized religion, the Bible has remained a cherished source of inspiration. Its scriptures contain timeless wisdom and beautiful passages that have guided my spiritual journey, reminding me to trust the Supreme.

From my standpoint, engaging with spiritual teachings, regardless of personal alignment with a specific religion, can offer valuable insights and guidance. By approaching these teachings with an open heart, you can draw wisdom from diverse sources to deepen your understanding of faith and spirituality. Trusting in a higher power provides comfort and strength, especially during hardship or uncertainty.

I don't speculate about the afterlife when I turn to the Bible. Instead, I seek encouragement and guidance for living well in the present moment. The scriptures are my anchor in need, offering solace and reassurance.

Furthermore, I understand that some people may dismiss the Bible for various reasons. However, my purpose here is not to convince anyone or prove my religiosity. Instead, I remind you that we do not control life's intricate processes. We cannot command our breath, heal ourselves, or orchestrate the world's natural cycles. Instead, we live in a universe that calls us to trust—trust in a force greater than ourselves.

I invite you to trust the Supreme for everything in your life, especially your emotional well-being. I am practicing this way of living, and I encourage you to join me in this step. Let us declare together that we will no longer live in fear. We are safe, secure, and supported in the Supreme's care.

The Variety of Spiritual Teachings

Just as there are many religions, there are many spiritual teachings. These teachings range from practical tips for a healthy life to profound insights, like the belief that God dwells within you. I began exploring some of these teachings in my 50s. Before then, I had no idea they existed. Here are just a few of the teachers whose messages resonate with me:

Viktor Frankl: Viktor Frankl was an Austrian neurologist, psychiatrist, and Holocaust survivor. His book, *Man's Search for Meaning,* found its way into my hands as I browsed the self-help shelves, desperately looking for hope. The book recounts Frankl's life and survival in Nazi concentration camps. One sentence grabbed me and helped me regain my balance:

Everything can be taken from a man but one thing: the last of the human freedoms—to choose one's attitude in any given set of circumstances, to choose one's own way.

Through observation, Frankl understood that while external circumstances—such as physical freedom, material possessions, and even life itself—can be taken away, one thing can never be stripped: the freedom to choose how we respond. This powerful idea, especially when I was weighed down by depression, brought a glimmer of hope, reminding me that even in the bleakest moments, I still had the power of choice.

Frankl's message reminded me that no matter how dire or uncontrollable a situation may be, we retain the power to choose our attitude, perspective, and the meaning we derive from the experience. Even in the concentration camps, where suffering was immense, Frankl saw that prisoners could control how they perceived their situation and how they responded to it. This ability to choose one's attitude, he believed, was integral to human dignity and psychological survival.

Frederick Douglass: Many people may not consider Frederick Douglass a spiritual thinker. Yet his *Narrative of the Life of Frederick Douglass, an American Slave*, offers a profound spiritual awakening. He describes the pivotal event: his fight against Edward Covey, a notorious "slave breaker."

Douglass had longed for freedom as a boy, but the brutal system of slavery nearly extinguished that desire. His resistance made him stand out to slaveholders, who sent him to Covey to break his spirit. For a time, it worked. Douglass admitted he had become "a slave in mind as well as body." But something awakened within him—a spiritual revelation of sorts. After his confrontation with Covey, Douglass reflected on what had happened:

I felt as if I had been emancipated from a living death. It was the first time I had ever fought, and the result of that fight gave me an insight into my own worth and showed me the strength of my resolve… At that moment, I determined that I would no longer live in the condition of an enslaved person. I resolved that if I could not be free by law, I would be free by force. I would be my own master, even if I had to die in the attempt.

This realization was transformative for Douglass. He understood he had been *born into slavery, then enslaved in mind*, but his newfound understanding of his worth set his mind free. In time, he also freed his body from the chains of slavery. He wrote, *I was now a man, and the determination to be free took root in my heart, and I was never again the same.*

Kitty Dukakis: While browsing the shelves in a bookstore, I came across *Now You Know: A Memoir* by Kitty Dukakis and Jane Scovell. I didn't know at the time that it delves into Kitty's struggles with depression and addiction, but I was drawn to its title, *Now You Know*. The emphasis on her mental health and spiritual journey deeply resonated with me, inspiring me with her resilience and determination.

Dukakis reflects on the challenges she faced in the public eye alongside her husband, a high-profile politician and presidential contender. She describes the emotional and psychological toll of public life and how it influenced her struggles. Her recovery journey involved not only medical treatments but also a deep introspection into her beliefs and values and a search for inner peace.

In later years, Dukakis openly discussed undergoing electroconvulsive therapy (ECT) for severe depression, calling it a life-saving measure. This decision demonstrated her profound commitment to healing and willingness to explore all avenues of spiritual and mental well-being.

While *"Now You Know"* does not explore specific spiritual practices or religious beliefs, it offers insight into Dukakis's resilience and pursuit of holistic healing. Her candor about her mental health struggles inspired me, giving me hope that emotional stability is possible.

While these biographies were inspiring, I began to dive deeper into spirituality around 2006. Admittedly, some of these teachings may seem bizarre to a Christian, but I kept an open mind to glean whatever I could from many sources. Perhaps the strangest of all are the teachings of Abraham. Esther Hicks is a dynamic and motivational public speaker, and she channels a collection of non-physical beings called Abraham, who share their wisdom with anyone asking questions.

Esther focuses on the principles of the Law of Attraction and the idea that we create our reality through our thoughts, feelings, and vibrations. These inspirational teachings would appeal to anyone interested in positive psychology and the practice of positive thinking. Here are a few points Esther emphasizes:

1. *You Are a Vibrational Being*: Everything in the universe, including you, is made up of energy and vibrates at a specific frequency. Your thoughts and emotions determine your vibrational tone.

2. *Law of Attraction*: Like attracts like, she says. Whatever you focus on—whether wanted or unwanted—manifests in your life. A positive focus attracts positive outcomes; a negative focus draws negativity.

3. *Emotional Guidance System*: Your emotions serve as a guide to your alignment with your desires. Feeling good indicates harmony with your inner being; negative emotions signal resistance.

In conveying the teachings of Abraham-Hicks, Esther emphasizes simplicity, positivity, and self-empowerment, encouraging followers to trust their inner guidance and embrace a life of ease and well-being. Esther shares these teachings in workshops throughout the United States and has written several books.

Two of Esther's most popular books, co-authored with her late husband Jerry, are:

1. *Ask and It Is Given: Learning to Manifest Your Desires.* This foundational book introduces Abraham's teachings and provides insights into the Law of Attraction. It includes practical exercises to help readers align with their desires and improve their vibration to manifest what they want.

2. *The Law of Attraction: The Basics of Abraham's Teachings.* This book distills the es-

sential principles of the Law of Attraction, as taught by Abraham. It serves as a guide to understanding how your thoughts and feelings shape your reality and how to create a fulfilling life deliberately.

Both books are highly regarded for their accessible explanations of spiritual principles and offer practical approaches to personal empowerment and manifestation.

While the teachings of Abraham are practical, Mooji's pointings are thoroughly spiritual. Mooji, born Anthony Paul Moo-Young, is a Jamaican-born expatriate to England. He comes from a Christian background, but his association with an Indian guru named Pappaji altered his perspective. Mooji's teachings are grounded in the Advaita Vedanta tradition, which emphasizes the concept of non-duality. He shares wisdom about self-realization and the possibility of awakening through direct experience, highlighting the nature of consciousness and the true Self. Some basic points in his teachings are as follows:

1. *True Self vs. Ego: Mooji emphasizes that our true nature is pure awareness or consciousness, existing* beyond the mind and ego. The ego, or the sense of a separate "I," is an illusion created by identification with thoughts and emotions.

2. *Self-Inquiry*: Besides Pappaji, Mooji is inspired by the teachings of Ramana Maharshi, who advocated self-inquiry as a path to self-realization. The key question is, "*Who am I?*" This practice helps strip away false identifications, revealing the eternal, unchanging awareness.

3. *The Present Moment*: Mooji stresses the importance of being fully present. He teaches peace and truth are found in the now, not past regrets or future expectations.

4. *Surrender and Trust*: Mooji encourages surrendering to life's flow, trusting that the universe supports our true being. Resistance stems from the ego, while acceptance brings peace.

Mooji shares his teachings through *Sat-sangs* (spiritual gatherings), many of which are held in Portugal and other countries in Western Europe and India. He is the author of *Before I Am: The Direct Recognition of Trust*, which emphasizes self-realization through discovering one's true nature. His other book, *White Fire: Spiritual Insights and Teachings of Advaita Zen Master Mooji*, synthesizes the teachings of Advaita Vedanta and Zen to guide us in understanding our true nature. Mooji is charismatic and offers humor as he shares his approach to discovering your true nature in simple and profound ways.

Many more spiritual teachers inspire me, some of whom I mentioned in this book. I've been on a path to resolve my emotional suffering for many years. This chapter gives a glimpse into some of the teachings I've studied and insights into how I live my life.

To break free from emotional distress, you'll need to find your way. The specific path does not matter. You may be Jew or Gentile, Protestant or Catholic, Muslim or Hindu, or anything else, but a system of faith is vital to feeling good. When all else fails, you'll need a place to anchor yourself as you navigate the emotional pain. As scripture exclaims, *Weeping may endure for a night, but joy comes in the morning.* Never give up because one day, you will break free from emotional distress.

Worksheet

Section 1: Reflecting on Life's Mystery

1. In your own words, describe what you think will happen when life ends. (Hint: Consider whether you view it as an end, a transformation, or something else.)

Response: _______________________________

____

____

____

Are there aspects of life you find mysterious? (For example, the cycle of life, your body's functioning, or the universe's vastness.)

Response: _______________________________

How does the concept of a Supreme Being or a higher power fit into your understanding of these mysteries?

Response: _______________________________

____

____

____

____

Section 2: Understanding "Nature's God"

1. The chapter discusses how many life functions happen without conscious control. List three examples of these automatic functions and describe how they inspire a sense of wonder. _______________

____

____

____

____

2. What role do you think a higher power plays in the natural processes of life and the earth? Consider elements such as food, water, or natural resources.

Response: _______________________________

____

____

____

Section 3: Finding Your Path

1. What spiritual or religious beliefs have influenced your perspective on life and the universe? (If none, reflect on what influences your perspective.)

Response: _______________________________

____

____

____

2. The chapter emphasizes finding a path that resonates with you. What steps can you

take to explore or deepen your spiritual beliefs?

Response: ___________________________

____

____

____

____

Section 4: Trust in the Supreme

1. How do you find comfort or strength during challenging times? (Do you rely on
   faith, prayer, meditation, or something
   else?)

Response: ___________________________

____

____

____

____

2. Write a short affirmation or prayer that reflects your trust in a higher power. Example: "I trust in the guidance of the Supreme, knowing I am supported and cared
   for in all things."

Your Affirmation: _______________________

____

____

____

____

Section 5: Reflecting on Key Teachings. Read each of the following quotes and answer the questions that follow.

1. Viktor Frankl: *"Everything can be taken from a man but one thing: the last of the human freedoms—to choose one's attitude in any given circumstances."*

- How does this idea apply to a current or past challenge in your life? _______________

____

____

____

- What small steps can you take to cultivate a positive attitude in challenging situations? _______________________

____

____

____

____

2. Frederick Douglass: *"I felt as if I had been emancipated from a living death."*

- What moments in your life have felt transformative? _______________________

  ____

  ____

  ____

- How did these moments shape your sense of self-worth or resolve? __________

  ____

  ____

  ____

3. Mooji: Mooji asks, *"Who am I?"* Spend 5 minutes reflecting and then write your thoughts.

- How does being fully present in the moment alter your perception of life's challenges? _______________________

____

____

____

____

Chapter 10

Accepting Myself

You have been criticizing yourself for years and it hasn't worked. Try approving of yourself and see what happens. Louise Hay

Accepting myself has been the most profound and challenging journey of my life. Living with a mental health condition often triggers a cascade of symptoms that disrupt both the mind and body. When the nervous system is out of balance, it can ignite a chain reaction of emotional and psychological turmoil.

Ordinary situations can begin to feel threatening, and fear may arise even when no real danger exists. You may find yourself blushing uncontrollably, withdrawing in social situations, or avoiding large crowds altogether. Over time, this fear can evolve into isolation, feeding on itself until even the most straightforward act, such as getting out of bed, feels insurmountable.

In the early 1980s, when my anxiety and depression spiraled out of control, I reached a breaking point. My fear became so overwhelming that even visiting my family—a place where I should have felt safe—brought discomfort. I vividly remember telling my mother, "I can't come home now." Mamma had already endured watching a daughter struggle with a mental health disorder; the idea of her son facing the same battle must have been unbearable. All she said was, "You sound down."

But I was nearly paralyzed by intense anxiety, and my fear of going home was a stark reminder of how disconnected I had become. At that moment, I realized that survival—simply being able to function—had to become my priority. Slowly but persistently, I battled my way back.

With time, patience, and determination, I began to experience moments of peace and clarity. I was fortunate to meet people who saw the best in me, offering a sense of connection and belonging that rekindled my confidence. As I continued my education, I found purpose and stability, and professional success became a source of reinforcement and hope.

One of the most important lessons I learned during this journey was the necessity of self-acceptance. Understanding the complexities of life and my struggles helped me see that accepting myself is not just vital—it's transformative. True acceptance means embracing the unique path life has laid before me, with all its pain, growth, and triumphs.

This isn't a battle against life or myself but a journey toward embracing and honoring my true self. As a friend puts it, *I am who I have become.* Or, as Michael Singer, author of *The Untethered Soul,* would say, as your ego self, *you are the sum total of your conditioning and life experiences.* This acceptance brings a sense of relief, a comforting realization that I am enough just as I am.

Loving What Is

Many modern-day teachers and writers urge us to accept ourselves. Byron Katie, author and founder of *The Work,* wrote a compelling book encouraging us to take life as it unfolds. *Loving What Is* was an instant bestseller when it came out in 1994, as people worldwide grappled with the meaning of life. Katie's core message is simple yet profound: suffering often arises not from our circumstances but from our resistance to them.

Katie teaches that the key to self-aceptance lies in questioning the thoughts and beliefs that keep us trapped in vicious cycles of self-judgment and dissatisfaction. Through her transformative method, *The Work*, Katie invites us to explore the stories we tell ourselves about who we are and how life should be. As Katie explains in her book, self-acceptance doesn't mean living passively or with resignation. Instead, it's about engaging with reality, not as we wish it to be.

This process of questioning and reframing our beliefs is liberating and empowering. It puts us in the driver's seat of our lives, enabling us to steer towards a more positive and acceptable view of ourselves. Her philosophy encourages us to ask: *Who would I be without this thought?* This question dismantles negative self-perceptions, opening the door to profound self-awareness and inner peace.

When I attended *The School for the Work* in 2008, I experienced firsthand how relentless Katie is about teaching us to accept the flow of life. I learned that self-acceptance is not about fixing ourselves but recognizing that there's nothing to fix. The stories we cling to—about not being good enough, smart enough, or lovable enough—are often just that: stories. Incorporating Katie's teachings into daily life can be a powerful tool for overcoming emotional distress. Her work reminds us that self-acceptance isn't a destination but a personal journey—a practice of meeting ourselves and others with kindness and honesty at every moment.

Katie's philosophy emphasizes that the thoughts we believe about ourselves are often the most significant barriers to inner peace. By gently questioning and reframing them, we can dismantle the mental constructs that keep us stuck in cycles of self-judgment and pain.

You're Not Broken

It's vital to recognize that you're not broken. But this truth may feel out of reach. Why? Because society, circumstances, and even our thoughts constantly tell us otherwise. The belief that you're broken doesn't arise overnight—it's often the result of repeated messages, internalized criticism, and unmet expectations. Over time, it becomes easy not only to believe you're broken but also to live as though that belief is a fact. But what if you challenged that story? What if, as Katie suggests, you questioned the thought, *I am broken*? Could it be that this idea isn't an inherent truth but a lens through which you've been taught to see yourself?

The good news is this lens can be adjusted and the story rewritten. Tools like self-reflection, journaling, and Katie's method of inquiry can help dismantle the belief in brokenness and replace it with the truth: you are whole, just as you are. These tools are not just helpful, they are essential in this journey of self-acceptance. They provide a roadmap, a way to navigate through our thoughts and beliefs, and a means to rewrite our story in a way that is more accepting and empowering.

Accepting yourself is about meeting yourself with love, curiosity, and grace. It's about recognizing that your worth is not contingent on perfection but on your existence. You were never broken, and knowing that is the first step to freedom. Consider these strategies to *break free* from emotional distress:

1. *Question the Thought*: When the belief "I am broken" surfaces, pause and ask yourself, "Is it true?" Follow Katie's method by digging deeper: "Can I know it's true?" Often, you'll find that the belief doesn't hold up under scrutiny.

2. *Reframe the Narrative*: Instead of seeing yourself as broken, try viewing yourself as a person who is growing, evolving, or learning. Every perceived "flaw" or "mistake" can be reframed as an opportunity for self-discovery and transformation.

3. *Practice Self-Compassion*: Treat yourself with the same kindness and understanding you would offer someone struggling, such as a close friend. Self-compassion can help quiet the inner critic and nurture a sense of worthiness.

Rewriting the Narrative of Brokenness

By challenging the thought "I am broken" and replacing it with kinder, more empowering beliefs, we begin to rewrite the story of our lives. The concept of brokenness was never about who we truly are. It stemmed from what we were taught to believe. Embracing the truth of our inherent worth creates the space to live more freely, authentically, and joyfully.

Few of us grow up with tools to recognize and dismantle our limiting beliefs, which often seem to emerge from nowhere, like whispers from the ether. When I went to college, I was filled with hope and promise, confident in my ability to make a positive contribution to society. I dreamed of becoming a lawyer, advocating for fairness and equity in the United States.

But somewhere along the way, negativity took root, and my self-esteem began to plummet. As I faced criticism and setbacks, self-doubt began to creep in. Over time, this doubt solidified into a pervasive belief: *I am not enough*. Eventually, this belief overpowered me. I saw myself as broken, and my inner circle mirrored that sense of worthlessness. Limiting beliefs, when carried, are often reinforced by those around us, unintentionally perpetuating a cycle of harm. This sense of inadequacy shaped my path, leading me on a journey of self-discovery and resilience that continues to this day.

In 2020, I launched a podcast called *The Possibility-Action Network* and adopted the moniker "Possibilityman." My life is a testament to what's possible with hope, faith, and determination. But before I became Possibilityman, I wrestled with the crushing weight of believing I was worthless. The refrain that I had aimed too high became constant in my mind.

Despite graduating with honors and earning a master's degree from a Big Ten university, I convinced myself that my education had been a mistake. I even considered abandoning my academic pursuits for trade school—not out of passion but fear. At my lowest point, I felt like an impostor, doubting my abilities despite evidence to the contrary. Unbelief weighed me down, clouding my perception of my potential. It wasn't until I turned to faith in God that I began to find strength and resilience. My faith became both a shield and a guide, helping me confront the lies I had internalized and rewrite my narrative.

With renewed determination, I returned to school to pursue a doctoral degree. It wasn't easy. For five years, I studied year-round while teaching full-time and raising a family. Hunger for change fueled me through countless challenges. That perseverance paid off. My academic credentials opened many doors to better opportunities, and my growing publication record eventually earned me the rank of full professor.

Today, my books are housed in libraries worldwide, and my journal articles serve as resources for students and researchers alike. I battled anxiety, depression, and isolation to reach this point. Yet, through it all, I emerged stronger and more resolute than ever. Possibilityman is not just a title; it's a testament to what's achievable when hope and determination guide the way. Each step forward, no matter how small, proves that we are never truly broken—only evolving.

Clouds of Witnesses

There are countless witnesses to the truth that our past or adverse experiences do not define us. These individuals remind us that challenges may shape our journey, but do not determine our destination. Their stories inspire us to rise above circumstances and embrace our boundless potential.

Growing up, I was surrounded by people who embodied resilience and determination—chief among them were my parents. They started with little but built a life that defied their humble beginnings. They worked from modest roots to owning a four-bedroom brick house with central heating and air. Despite his lack of formal education, my father became a steadfast laborer, while my mother inspired us with her dreams and determination. Together, they raised eight children with limited resources yet never let us go hungry. Their sacrifices taught me the true meaning of perseverance.

Another towering figure in my life was my uncle. Although born with physical challenges, uncle understood two essential truths: adversity is inevitable but can be transcended. Standing under five feet tall and walking with a noticeable waddle, he faced obstacles that would have daunted most. Yet, he never allowed these challenges to define him.

As a young man, uncle sought work in lumber mills, where men of larger stature often tried to push him aside. Refusing to give up, he caught the foreman's attention with his persistence and was eventually hired. That opportunity transformed his life.

He later secured a stable job, bought a truck, married, and raised successful children. Uncle often said, "Take what you got and make what you want," and "Can't been dead; I buried the scoundrel." Despite his lack of formal education, uncle acquired land, leaving a legacy for his children. He was a living testament to resilience and resourcefulness, inspiring everyone who knew him. His life reinforced a truth I carry: we are not broken. We are becoming.

Seven Sacred Truths

No matter what you've done or haven't done, you've punished yourself enough. It's time to stop. Internet

One day, you will awaken to the truth: you are now the person you were destined to be. You've been clinging to false beliefs and relying on others to shape your life. But now, it's time to make a courageous decision and declare: *If it's to be, it's up to me.*

As I began to focus on my gifts and talents rather than on others, I progressively let go of the patterns of thinking, acting, and perceiving holding me back. Of course, it wasn't easy. There were countless hurdles along the way. But the more I embraced my humanity, acknowledging my strengths and weaknesses, the more I let go of the weight of so-called mistakes and began to live in the blessings that naturally flowed into my life.

Furthermore, you didn't make mistakes alone. Life is interconnected, and circumstances and the people around you influence your decisions. You are not alone in this journey; understanding this can bring a sense of unity and shared experience.

While I deeply regret anyone who was hurt by my actions, I reject the narrative that I am inherently flawed or unworthy. Self-blame is a heavy burden; you must let it go when it becomes too much. Rejecting self-blame is not a sign of weakness but a powerful act of self-compassion and empowerment.

To fully accept yourself and align with your rightful path, plant these seven sacred truths in your spirit:

1. *You made the best decision you could at the time*: If you truly knew better, you would have made a better decision. Some people lack empathy, but you are not one of them. If you were, you wouldn't carry the burden of regret or feel the sting of your missteps.

2. *Everyone has regrets, even if they hide them*: I once shared my sorrows with a relative, a man who seemed proud of his life despite significant struggles. He had faced financial instability, failed relationships, and the challenges of providing for his children. Yet, he chose to focus on his successes rather than his setbacks.

His story reminded me that no one lives a perfect life. People may judge and avoid you, but they also have flaws and regrets. Accept this truth: judgment from others often says more about them than it does about you.

3. *Stop complaining about your mistakes*: You've never made mistakes—you've had learning experiences. The key question is: *Did you learn from them?* If yes, those experiences were valuable. Embracing the value of learning from experiences can shift your perspective from regret to optimism and growth.

I once believed that complaining about my past was therapeutic. It isn't. Instead, it poisoned the minds of those who listened and mine. Seek out "lightworkers" who see the best in you and help you uncover your untapped potential. They'll guide you toward your tribe, your soul family, who will support and grow with you.

4. *Distance yourself from those who put you down*: At my lowest, I surrounded myself with people who criticized me. Even my pastor once told me something was inherently wrong with me. I later told a friend what he had said, and without hesitation,

she replied, "Something is wrong with him."

It took someone else to remind me that his harsh words reflected his inner struggles, not mine. When you allow others to dishonor you, you dishonor yourself. To accept yourself, you must honor who you are. You're worthy—now and always. You don't have to allow anyone to abuse you—walk away.

5. *Others cannot make you happy*: Happiness doesn't come from others; it comes from within. As Michael Singer explains in *The Untethered Soul,* the positive emotions you associate with someone else are generated by your nervous system, brain, experiences, and inner processes.

   Happiness isn't something others can create for you. It's already within you, waiting to be discovered and nurtured.

6. *Recognize your divine nature*: Yes, you are made in the image of God, however you

conceive the Absolute to be. This truth isn't about your body, personality, or memories. It's about your awareness—your consciousness. That spark of awareness is your connection to the divine.

You've been taught to see yourself as weak or sinful, but it's time to reclaim your power. You are capable, valuable, and deeply connected to the Source of all creation.

7. *Seek balance in your life*: Buddhism teaches the Middle Way, a path of moderation. Extremes, whether high or low, often lead to imbalance. True freedom and happiness come from embracing balance in every aspect of life.

   Avoid lofty expectations of yourself or others. Instead, strive for harmony. The Middle Way empowers you to achieve your goals while remaining grounded and fulfilled.

So, remember, whenever you feel anxious, depressed, or overwhelmed, it's because you're believing something untrue. Just as a mechanic identifies a rough engine as needing a tune-up or grinding iron needs grease, your emotions also signal misalignment. The solution? Breathe. Slow down. Stop. Reconnect with the truth of who you are: a divine being forever connected to your Source.

You've mastered surviving.
It's time to live now. Internet

Epilogue

As I bring this guide and journey to a close, I'd like to share a truth that may not be what you expect. The title of this book, *Break Free from Emotional Distress*, might suggest that freedom is a permanent state, a finish line you cross and never look back. But my reality is more nuanced and, I dare say, more human.

While I have achieved emotional balance, it is not a static achievement. Balance is a dynamic process requiring daily attention and care. The tools and insights I've shared in these pages are not one-time fixes. They are lifelong companions, practices to be revisited, refined, and relied upon whenever the storms of life gather again. And they will gather in one form or another. That's the nature of living.

I've learned that breaking free does not mean breaking away from all challenges or feelings of distress. It means finding the strength and the strategies to navigate through them. It means recognizing the signs when old patterns resurface and having the courage to confront them head-on. It means embracing the messy, imperfect, and deeply rewarding work of self-care and self-awareness.

In writing this book, I've opened up about my struggles with depression, anxiety, fear and the ways I sabotaged my happiness. I've shared my journey through marriage, divorce, and the moral injuries that left scars I once thought would never heal. These experiences have shaped me, but they do not define me. What defines me now is my commitment to my health and well-being and the hope that my story can inspire others to embark on their healing journeys.

If you've made it this far, thank you for walking alongside me in these pages. I hope you've found tools that resonate with you, practices that feel doable, and genuine encouragement. I hope you see it's okay to stumble, struggle, and seek help. There is no shame in the ongoing work of healing.

Perhaps you can draw encouragement from the words of Sugar Ray Robinson, a boxing icon. Born Walker Smith Jr. in 1921, he was one of the greatest boxers in history, widely regarded as the best pound-for-pound fighter of all time. Known for his exceptional speed, power, agility, and charisma, Robinson had an illustrious boxing career, becoming a world champion in both the welterweight and middleweight divisions. He held a professional record of 174 wins, 19 losses, 6 draws, and 109 knockouts, with an incredible 91-fight unbeaten streak early in his career.

Robinson wrote his autobiography, The Fight of My Life, with Herb Goldman in 1969, providing readers with insights into his life inside and outside the ring. He reflected on his journey of overcoming personal battles. He wrote candidly about the discipline it took to excel as an athlete and rebuild himself after moments of failure and doubt. Robinson emphasized that the fight for well-being is daily, requiring vigilance, humility, and consistent effort. Whether through physical fitness, mental focus, or nurturing his relationships, his approach to life is a reminder that greatness—any form—is not a destination, but a continual journey.

May his story serve as a reminder to you and me. Like Robinson, we are all in a daily fight—not necessarily in a boxing ring but in the arena of life. Each day brings opportunities to care for us, stay attuned to our needs, and make choices that align with our values and goals. Some days will be more challenging than others, and that's okay. What matters is showing up, again and again, for yourself.

Thank you for being part of this journey. May your path forward be one of growth, courage, and self-compassion. And may you find strength in the daily walk, knowing that every small step you take is a victory worth celebrating.

Further Reading

Balsekar, R. (1993). *The Ultimate Understanding.* Advaita Press.

Banks, Sydney. (1998). *The Missing Link: Reflections on Philosophy & Spirit.* International Human Relations Consultants, Inc.

Beers, C. W. (1908). *A Mind that Found Itself: An Autobiography.* Longmans, Green & Co.

Burns, D. D. (1990). *The Feeling Good Handbook.* Plume Printing.

Burns, D. D. (2020). *Feeling Great: The Revolutionary New Treatment for Depression and Anxiety.* PESI Publishing & Media.

Borders, P. B., et al (2022). *Micro shift: Small Mindset Changes for Big Results. Amazon.*

Caerlang, A. (2017). *A Reminder for You When You've Made So Many Mistakes in Life.* Thought Catalog. thoughtcatalog.com.

Chapman, G. D. (2015). *The 5 Love Languages: The Secret to Love That Lasts.* Northfield Publishing.

Diaz, D. S. (2023). *Gasping for air: The Stranglehold of Narcissistic Abuse.* Delaney's Heart Publications.

Dispenza, J. (2007). *Evolve Your Brain: The Science of Changing Your Mind.* Health Communications, Inc.

Dwoskin, H. (2003). *The Sedona Method: Your Key to Lasting Happiness, Success, Peace and Emotional Well-being.* Sedona Press.

Dyer, W. (1976). *Your Erroneous Zones: Step-by-step Advice for Escaping the Trap of Negative Thinking and Taking Control of Your Life.* Funk & Wagnalls.

Dunkley, B. (2021). *Ultimate Mind Hacking: 16 Highly Effective ways to Smash Your Unhealthy Thought Patterns.* Independently published.

Epictetus. (1890). *The Discourses of Epictetus: With the Enchiridion and Fragments* (G. Long, Trans.). G. Bell and Sons.

Goldman, H. (1969) and Sugar Rayu Robinson. *The Fight of my Life.* Coward-McCann.

Hicks, E. (2004). *Ask and it is Given: Learning to Manifest Your Desires.* Hay House.

Higginson, T. W. (1890). *The Works of Epictetus: His Discourses, in Four Books, Enchiridion, and Fragments.* Thomas Nelson and Sons.

Hooks, E. (2025) "Saying 'Yes' Too Quickly." In *Does It Matter*, March 14.

Levenson, L. (1993). *Keys to the ultimate freedom: Thoughts and talks on personal transformation.* Sedona Press.

Katie, B. (2001). *Loving What Is: Four Questions That Can Change Your Life.* Three Rivers Press.

Katie, B. (2007). *A Thousand Names for joy: Living in Harmony with the way Things are.* Harmony Books.

Kunjufu, J. (1998). *Sankofa: Stories of Power, Hope, and Joy.* Pennsylvania State University Press.

Langer, E. J. (2023). *The Mindful Body: Thinking our way to Chronic Health.* Ballantine Books.

Louder, P. (2021). *Living Louder: A Compassionate Journey Through Federal Prison.* Blake Street.

Low, A. (1954). *Mental Health Through will Training.* Christopher Publishing House.

Mooji. (2011). *Before I Am: The Direct Recognition of Trust.* Mooji Media.

Mooji. (2015). *White Fire: Spiritual Insights and Teachings of Advaita Zen Master.* Mooji Media.

Mowat, B. A. (2012). *Hamlet by William Shakespeare.* Simon & Schuster.

North, R. (n.d.). "Our Brains Are Wired for Connection. *The Minds Journal.* Retrieved April 8, 2025, from https://themindsjournal.com/quotes/our-brains-are-wired-for

Perry, B. D. (2006). *The Boy Raised as a Dog: And Other Stories From a Child Psychiatrist's Notebook.* Basic Books.

Prather, H. (1970). *Notes to Myself: My Struggle to Become a Person.* Fawcett.

Rau, N., & Rau, M. (1971). *My Dear Ones: The Love Story of a Great Physician for his Patients.* Prentice Hall.

Rosenberg, M. B. (2015). *Nonviolent Communication: A Language of life: Life-changing tools for Healthy Relationships* (3rd ed.). PuddleDancer Press.

Rozin, P., & Royzman, E. B. (2001). "Negativity Bias, Negativity Dominance, and Contagion." *Personality and Social Psychology Review,* 5(4), 296-32.

Sapolsky, R. M. (2023). *Determined: A Science of Life Without Free Will.* Penguin Random House.

Schwartz, A. (2021). *The Fawn Response: Understanding and Healing Trauma Through the Parasympathetic Nervous System.* Sounds True.

Teevens, C. (2013). *The Happiness Lie.* Go Beyond.

Teevens, C. (2009). *Alchemy: How To Feel Good No Matter What.* GoBeyond.

Tolle, E. (1997). *The Power of Now: A Guide to Spiritual Enlightenment.* New World Library.

Winfrey, O., & Perry, B. D. (2021). *What Happened to you? Conversations on Trauma, Resilience, and Healing.* Flatiron Books.

Ziglar, Z. (1977). *See You at the Top.* Pelican Publishing Company.